NICOLE HECK

A Saint For Life

Copyright © 2016 Nicole Heck

All rights reserved.

ISBN: 1518630693
ISBN-13: 978-1518630699

This book is dedicated to my dear friend Jen Luft. I hold my friendship with you close to my heart. Your strength through your battle inspires me. Stay strong and never give up.

In loving memory of my grandmother, Margaret Lanci, and my friend, Alex Held.

Acknowledgements

Writing my first novel was a goal I never thought I would accomplish at such a young age. It was a dream I couldn't foresee in my near future. This book wasn't just a two year journey, it started from the very first day I decided I wanted to be an author and along the way there have been so many people who have helped me get to this point.

First, I couldn't have done this without the support from my family. From day one as a young writer, they have been nothing but encouraging and positive about my dream to publish a book, especially my parents. I want to express my sincere gratitude toward my Mom, Dad, brother, sister, grandparents, aunts, uncles, and cousins. Thank you for believing in me, in my work, and supporting my dream. I am so blessed to have such a loving family.

Thank you to my wonderful and talented editor Anna at Polished Arrow Editing. Thank you for taking a chance on me as an author and having the patience to work with me. Your comments and advice helped me get through writer's block and overall improved my book as a whole. I could not have done this without you.

To my cover designers at LSDdesign. Thank you for doing an incredible job and being so quick to make changes if I needed them.

I owe a huge thank you to my best friend Kayla. From spending long days at Starbucks with me while I wrote, reading through chapters, and giving me opinions, being understanding and helpful when I suffered from writer's block, and listening to my new ideas, I couldn't have done it without you. Thank you for being with me through every step of this process.

To Kristen, Kelsey, John, Katharina, Megan, Dillon, and Katherine; I am so privileged to be able to call all of you my closest friends. Whether you have been in my life for just a year, or eight years, each and every one of you have been amazing friends to me. Thank you for being so supportive, inspiring, or- just being there for me when I needed someone.

During part of this journey, I worked for a gym in Raleigh, North Carolina. I soon realized that I was meant to cross paths with some of my co-workers for a reason. When I struggled to write, they kept me going. The support and encouragement they passed on to me was overwhelming at times. To Logan, Ricky, Taylor, Ana, and Natalia, thank you for being so accepting of my dream and for believing in me.

To Stu and the Pack family, thank you for believing in me and for instilling confidence in me that I could go after my dreams without failure. You were both there for me when I decided to make choices that would take me down a different road in life. Without your help, I would never have been able to make it as far as I have. I was scared and you helped me to believe in myself and guided me to make decisions that was right for my future.

To the Spagnola family, Josh Gardiner, Josh Nethaway, Ronnie Bernick, and the rest of the Mohawks family; thank you for being there for me when I needed it the most, for being great friends, and for supporting me in various ways along my journey.

To the Held family; I can't express deeply enough how grateful I am to have people like you in my life. Your support for my goals and dreams means more to me than I can describe. Alex was the first person I told about the idea for this book. His words of encouragement helped me get started. He left footprints on my heart. I will be forever grateful to have had him in my life.

To Mrs. Bartyzel, Mrs. Carmichael, and Professor Cotler; thank you for supporting my passion for writing, for believing in my writing, and for helping me to become a better writer. If it wasn't for the support from teachers like you, I would have given up at some point along the way. You helped me to believe that I was capable of turning my words into something meaningful.

Last but certainly not the least, to the entire Development and Athletics staff at Siena. Without your guidance, support, or inspiration, none of this would be possible. I come to work each day grateful to work for and with some of the most amazing people. Not everyone is this lucky to love their job. I am so blessed to have been given the opportunity I have and I will forever be indebted to all of you for the support you've given me.

Thank you to everyone who chooses to pick up my book and read it. My wish for you is that you'll take one step forward toward a dream you've always wanted to achieve, that'll while looking at my book you'll believe in yourself again, that you'll believe in the goodness of the world, that there's love and beauty in everything that surrounds you, and lastly that you won't let anyone or any of life's setbacks, set you back.

{1}

Zoe

"How much longer do we have to wait? I'm hungry," Gabe asked.

I checked my watch. I was hungry too, but since the doctors were keeping us waiting, I'm not sure I'm going to have time to get breakfast before class.

"I don't know. I thought they would have checked in on us by now. I'll tell you what: because I'm such a good sister, I'll drive to Dunkin' Donuts, and if and only if there's no line, you can get a bagel before—"

Two knocks on the door interrupted my sentence. Dr. Sheehan walked in along with an unfamiliar face. Gabe tapped me on the shoulder and smiled. There wasn't a bit of worry on his face. He was more optimistic than me about this appointment.

"Maybe I can go to the next Siena game?" he whispered.

"Maybe!" I tried to remain positive. Going to a Siena game is all he's wanted to do.

"So, Gabe," Dr. Sheehan spoke up but swallowed and seemed to choke on her words. "How are you feeling today?"

"I was really tired yesterday, but I'm not today!" He sat there kicking his legs against the table and smiling cheerfully.

1

"Good. I'm so happy to hear that!" She turned to the unfamiliar face we had yet to be introduced to. "This is my new intern. Gabe, is it okay if he does our usual routine testing on you while I chat with Zoe in my office?"

"Sure thing!"

I couldn't seem to find the floor as I stood up and almost fell. She needed to talk to me by myself, which could only mean one thing—bad news.

Dr. Sheehan could barely look me in the eyes. In fact, I could see the tears starting to fall behind her glasses before she even spoke, and when she did, her words made my heart ache.

"I'm so sorry, Zoe. We're trying everything we can. I was really optimistic that this time…that this time…" She held her hands to her face. "I'm sorry. Gabe is one of my favorite patients, and I just love you guys. I hate to see him suffering. I wish I could have told you today that the cancer was gone, but the cancer cells are growing even more rapidly than they were before."

"I understand. It's not your fault. What do we do now?"

"There's another clinical trial I would like him to try. That way it comes at no cost to you."

"What results have you seen from this trial? Do you think it will work?"

"I'm fairly optimistic. He has a chance. We've given the treatments to only a few children, and for most, there was a significant decrease in the cancer cells in their body. It's a very safe treatment. Although there's a risk as there is with everything but we haven't lost a patient yet."

"Let's do it. And what about a bone marrow transplant? Is there any more hope in finding a donor?"

"Gabe is on the list."

"So I just have to keep praying we'll find a match?" I sighed.

"We're going to do everything we can."

As Gabe and I walked out of the hospital, he reached for my hand.

"Zoe, it's going to be okay. I'm fine. Don't worry! I'm just sick, but I'll get better. You heard Dr. Sheehan. She knows I can beat this."

If only I had as much confidence as he did. I bent down to give him a hug. "That's right. You will beat this! I love you, kiddo."

"I love you too."

The drive home was silent. I felt hopeless. Looking in the rearview mirror, I glanced at Gabe, who had fallen asleep within minutes of driving away from the hospital. I wish there was more I could do for him.

*

I used the saliva on my cold fingers to wipe away the black mascara that smeared underneath my red and puffy eyes. After I dropped Gabe off at home, it became hard for me to stop crying.

Watching everyone pass by, I headed toward Siena Hall and considered skipping class. I didn't want to see or talk to anyone today, but I had no choice.

I reached for my new Starbucks cup and took a sip of my horribly strong French vanilla coffee. The consistency could never turn out right for me. Taking a deep breath, I exited my warm car into the crisp air.

"It's going to be okay. I don't look like a hot mess. I won't see anyone important. It could be worse," I said aloud.

The chapel bells rang. I looked down at my watch only to realize that I was now late for class. So much for making it on time. I sighed.

Looking around at my surroundings, I didn't notice anyone other than a few stragglers like myself. I looked into the side mirror of my car, brushed back a few stray hairs, and wiped away the tears that were left in the corner of my eye. Quickly applying a coat of mascara over my wet eyelashes, I finally began the trek across the parking lot covered in melting snow.

I slowed down my pace as soon as I approached the building.

Rushing didn't seem necessary anymore considering I would already be marked late. A few more minutes wouldn't make a difference. I felt my phone vibrating in my purse that was tucked away under my shoulders up against my ribs. Sliding one strap off of my shoulder, I reached in for my phone. I had several notifications. I didn't even realize that it had gone off. My mind was in a fog ever since the words I dreaded hearing rolled off of Dr. Sheehan's tongue.

The thought of losing the only family that was still in my life horrified me. The cancer cells are growing even faster, and if this trial doesn't work, what will? Will Gabe beat this? I found it harder to breathe as my anxiety heightened. I sat down on the closest bench along the sidewalk and let my short breaths appear before me as I exhaled and rubbed my hands together, increasing the friction to give off some heat. I could barely see. My heart rate had skyrocketed. I laid my head down into the palms of my hands, closed my eyes, and took deeper breaths to try and talk myself out of it. I took a water bottle out of my purse and slowly drank it until finally my anxiety subsided.

I continued to walk along the path. The melting snow on either side of the pavement reminded me of when my father would take me to get ice cream every Sunday afternoon. After church we'd come home, change our clothes, pack our bikes in the car, and head over to the bike path. The two of us would ride to a small magical place in the middle of nowhere.

I envisioned sunflowers filling up the quad along with tall weeds and vegetables. Over my left shoulder, the dining hall, in my mind, became a small brick building where people were lining up with their families at the order window. My dad and I would take our helmets off and place them on our favorite picnic table. Somehow it was always unoccupied. I would sit there patiently waiting for him to bring back my ice cream—hot fudge covering the entire scoop of cookies and cream ice cream, a little bit of whipped cream on top, and my favorite part, the cookie crumbs sprinkled all over. My dad, Anderson Gingras, was a plain guy, much different from myself. A scoop of vanilla on a waffle cone was always his choice.

After we finished, he would have to wipe off the leftover fudge that remained on my chin. "Saving some for the ride?" he would say, causing us to laugh for a few minutes. The rays from the sun would begin to beam down on us, and the smiles had become permanent fixtures on our faces. It was the perfect picture.

I missed him so much, even more so on days like today. A film of tears was starting to cover my eyes again when I knocked into somebody. My cup and phone dropped out of my hand, landing on the wet pavement before me.

"I am so sorry. I wasn't paying attention to where I was going. I'm out of it. I'm sorry!" the young guy said while picking up my phone.

I looked him in the eye. I knew him. I didn't know him personally, but I knew all too well who he was.

Without saying a word, I grabbed my phone and walked away hurriedly. I didn't want him to see me crying or embarrass myself any more than I already had. For the very first time, I hope that in that mere moment he didn't know who I was.

{2}

Christian

I ran through the parking lot next to the baseball field, weaving in and out of snow-covered cars and then sprinted up the hill next to the science building. I was close enough now where I could see the doors and the window to my classroom. Living on the opposite side of campus was a challenge when I had early classes.

I checked the time, I guessed that I had approximately three minutes to make it all the way there before my professor finished taking attendance.

Nope, I have to run. I took a deep breath and continued.

The bottoms of my sweatpants were getting wetter as my feet submerged into the puddles of melting snow. Just then, my chances of getting to class before being late dropped significantly. Her cup fell to the ground, spilling coffee everywhere, and her phone dropped onto the wet ground in front of us. It barely missed a puddle.

"I am so sorry. I wasn't paying attention to where I was going. I'm out of it. I'm sorry." Somehow I found myself apologizing even though I wasn't the only one at fault. I stopped myself from talking after noticing that she hadn't said a word. I was rambling on now, which was appearing to make the situation worse.

I reached my arm out to give her phone back to her. She grabbed it from my hands aggressively, and when she looked me in the eye everything around us seemed to pause. In that moment I felt an immediate sense of familiarity. The innocence of her gentle smile and the glassiness of her eyes made me long to feel again. Her mouth slightly opened, but before she could say anything, she turned around and walked away. She didn't look back. Her speed increased progressively, and she disappeared into the building, leaving the doors behind her swinging against the bricks.

I tried to process what had just happened but I couldn't move. She didn't even say a word. When she looked me in the eye, it didn't seem to faze her.

"Hi, Chris!" A girl I didn't recognize walked by and smiled.

"Hi," I subtly replied and started to slowly walk to class. It was normal for me that random people were always saying hello or striking up a conversation. I've never had a girl blatantly ignore me. This was a first.

After slowly making it up the stairs to the second floor, my eyes caught sight of her again. I peeked into the classroom as I walked by. She was slipping her jacket off of her back, but as she turned around the professor shut the door before I could see her face again. She looked so familiar, but I couldn't figure out where I knew her from. Maybe I hooked up with her before? Maybe I didn't even know her? Maybe she doesn't know who I am? Although, I am—

"Christian Michaels, what took you so long?" My professor interrupted my thoughts.

"Sorry, it won't happen again." I closed the door behind me.

"Please see me after class. "

I nodded.

I sat down next to my roommate, the huge grin plastered across his face was hard to miss.

"Why were you so late this morning?" Matthew laughed.

"Yeah, thanks for waking game up!" This wasn't the first time he's failed to wake me up if I've fallen back to sleep. He thought it was funny, mostly because he knew no teacher would actually punish me, but this professor seemed to be stricter than most.

"Sorry, I just thought you decided to skip because you didn't finish the paper." He snickered.

"Paper? What paper?" Sheer panic resided inside me now.

"The paper that was on the syllabus. He mentioned it at the end of the last class." Matt pointed to the page where it was listed.

Truth is I didn't even look at the syllabus yet. Sure enough, there it was. Assignment number 3. "Number 3? What were the first two assignments? The semester just started."

Our professor shot us a look to stop talking. I read over the syllabus while he was teaching. How could I already be three assignments behind? Hopefully I'll be able to hand them in late. I can't afford three zero's.

"Dude, you alright? What happened to you when you went home for Christmas? Do you need a drink?" Matt whispered to me. He thought a drink was the answer to everything, but in his defense, in the past I've tried to cover up my grief with alcohol or girls instead of facing it. I don't want to hide my grief anymore.

"No, that won't help. It's about my brother. That's all."

That ended the conversation. As good of a friend as Matt was, he never wanted to talk about James. I don't blame him. Nobody wants to start their day off talking to someone about their dead brother. But that's just it. Nobody here wants to talk about it.

I finally opened up my notebook and put my pen to the paper, but the next thing I knew, class was over. Looking down, I had written nothing. It was hard for me to pay attention when all I could think about was that I'm already failing in my promise to James—my promise to do well and succeed in everything I do. Everything he never got a chance to do.

I lingered until almost everyone was on their way to other classes and made my way to the front of the classroom.

"Mr. Michaels, at the beginning of the semester I usually give students one pass. I'm not sure I can give three."

"Please. I'll get them to you by the next class, I promise," I said.

I'm not sure if it was because I had despair in my voice or because our basketball team would be in trouble if I didn't have a good GPA, but he gave me a second chance.

I took mental notes of everything I needed to get done tonight on my way to practice. I walked the longer route to kill some time.

Walking past Ryan Hall, a particular window with a flag hanging on the wall inside stuck out to me. That room was my brother's dorm room for a few short days. James was killed in a tragic accident his first week here. It was my decision to honor his memory and go to school here. I wanted to make my brother proud. I don't think he would be too happy if he knew I was slacking off in my last semester.

As I entered into the locker room, the silence of being early let me be alone with my thoughts. I took out my practice gear and sat down on the bench.

Placing my muddy sneakers at the bottom of my locker, my mind drifted to my run in this morning with the girl with the red cup. Someone as stunningly angelic as her was hard to forget. I couldn't shake the feeling inside of me that's telling me that we ran into each other for a reason, that it was meant to happen. She made me want to feel again and to fill the void in my life that I even didn't realize I had. Thinking about this mystery girl was the only thing that made me forget about how much I missed having an older brother.

{3}

Zoe

"So did I hear you correctly, or am I delusional? Christian Michaels ran straight into you. *The* Christian Michaels."

I nodded.

"The one you've had a crush on since freshman year. And you didn't even say a word? Are you sick?" Emily stopped in front of the arena and felt my forehead. "This is just not normal."

"I froze, Em. I didn't know what to do."

"You had such a prime opportunity to talk to him, and you blew it just like that!"

I sighed. "Well, it doesn't matter. He stopped talking to me once he looked me in the eye."

"Oh, stop."

"What was I going to say anyway? I would have stuttered. It would have been even more embarrassing." I hastily said back to her.

"You are you, if that makes any sense at all."

"That says a lot."

"It does! You are amazing!"

"I would hardly say that."

"You've just had bad luck in the past."

"Really, really bad luck." I sighed again.

"Well, maybe this is fate. Maybe this is the moment I have been telling you will come for a while now! Maybe he'll see you tonight!" Emily was all fired up about her theory, that the perfect guy for me was going to come into my life this year. Tonight we were working at the basketball game. We both worked for the athletic department for our work study.

Emily tugged at my hand. "Come on, let's go! We're going to be late!"

"I'm just a little nervous. What if he recognizes me, the girl who spilled her coffee all over herself? I had been crying all morning, so I looked awful too!"

"It was his fault though. Not the crying, but you know what I mean. You should talk to him after the game today," she suggested.

"And say what, exactly? I don't know, Emily. Can we just stop talking about it?"

"Okay, okay." Emily shook her head and continued to walk.

"He's seen me, but he's never noticed me. He's never looked twice. Remember I had a class with him a few semesters ago?"

"Yeah, and every time you saw him you got the feeling that you needed to talk to him, remember?"

"Whatever. It's just a stupid crush."

"Can I just say one thing?" Emily stopped and turned around.

"Go ahead," I mumbled.

"You have been in love with him since the day you walked onto this campus. If the opportunity strikes again, please promise me you won't bail."

"Why?" I asked. I always wondered why she invested so much time into my love life. We were very different people when it came to feelings and relationships.

"I just want you to see what happens. You need a good guy in your life. It doesn't hurt to try. All you have to do is say hi. One step at a time. Better you than me, anyway. You know I don't like this kind of stuff. Having to go on dates scares me."

"That's true, I guess. I don't know. I'll see." At this point I was agreeing with her to get her to drop the subject.

We walked into the arena and our boss called us over. As we were walking over toward her, Christian ran out onto the court. My stomach sank, and I hurried to where he wouldn't see me.

"Our social media worker came down with the flu. Would you mind being a rock star and providing the updates on the Twitter page for the game today? Emily, I am going to have you working on the concourse." My boss finished giving directions, and I looked over at Emily. This would be one of the first games we weren't working side by side.

"Yeah, that's not a problem. I can do that. The computer is set up at the tables behind the hoop, right?" I asked my boss, but the words slowly drifted out of my mouth as I watched Christian warm up on the court. Each time he ran the ball down the court, he never missed a shot. Each basket was flawless. His incredible talent overpowered everyone else out on the court, so much that even the opposing team stopped to watch.. They stood there with anger and frightened looks upon their faces. They knew what they were up against.

"We had to change it up today because of a blown fuse. The computer's set up at the scorer's table. It's right next to the Siena bench. The thing only took us a few hours to get it all straight. Thankfully I had everything else done." Her words went in one ear and out the other. I couldn't take my eyes off of the court.

"Okay, great. I will head over there in a minute." I shrugged and noticed that Emily was smirking at me.

"Awesome. I knew I could count on you!" she said while rushing off.

"I was trying so hard not to LOL through that entire conversation." Emily laughed.

"Stop. This isn't funny."

"Yes, it is. See? It's meant to be. Now's your time."

"Bye, Em." I quietly laughed along with her. This would be

my luck. My brain finally processed what she had asked me to do.

My anxiety shot through the roof. Of all days, this was too coincidental. This means I would have to sit right next to the Siena bench. I would be front and center where Christian could see me.

Maybe he won't remember me?

Thoughts were running through my mind endlessly.

He definitely won't remember me. Why would he? He never has before.

I walked over to where she told me to go, trying my best to avoid eye contact with him. I moved my hair to the right side of my face to hide my eyes as I walked by. Luckily the game was about to start. The team lined up for the Star Spangled Banner.

I glanced up from my computer and looked over at him only to notice that he was staring right at me. I put my head back down. Looking back up for a brief second, we held eye contact this time.

Shit, no, look away; look away I kept repeating to myself over and over in my head. He smiled at me. I looked down at the computer then up and to the right. When I gazed back in his direction, he was looking straight forward and not at me anymore.

"What just happened?" I said under my breath and let out a sigh of relief. The clock ran down to the buzzer, and the crowd stood as the little girl who stood at center court started to sing the national anthem.

I couldn't help but continue glancing at him while she sang, and I began noticing all of his attractive features in a new way. Good thing he was in the same direction as the flag so it didn't look so obvious. With sandy blonde hair, from behind he reminded me of a young Lucas Scott from One Tree Hill. His upper body was very muscular. I could see his veins in his forearms as he stood with his back toward me, hands clasped behind him. Underneath the white and green uniform, I imagined the rest of his body was just as defined.

I didn't even realize the national anthem had ended until I seemed to be the last one standing in the entire arena. I was in a zone admiring Christian from afar. I kept replaying the events that had occurred when he ran into me and just now when he clearly recognized me.

He recognized me. For a moment a brief smile appeared on my face.

{4}

Christian

Through the snowflakes falling from the gray sky, I found myself drifting off into a peaceful state of mind. Music played loudly in my ear, and I tried to shift my focus to the game tonight. The black pavement was now covered in a sheet of white. The snow had been accumulating for the last hour.

As I laid my head on the window, we slowly approached the arena. I was watching the cars pass by when my eyes drifted toward two girls walking up the steps. I tried not to stare, but the girl in the back caught my attention. All of her hair was resting over her right shoulder, and she walked in a way which seemed familiar. A sudden moment of anxiousness ran through my body until she was no longer in my sights.

Was it red cup girl? I didn't know what else to call her. She comes to the games? She sure made a lasting imprint on me.

*

It was refreshing to see all of the support we had as a team as I stepped out into the arena. I looked around and bumps rose on my bare arms when I noticed that most of the fans were wearing shirts with my number on them. Each game the number of fans appeared to increase, which continued to give me more encouragement to play my absolute best.

Running to the side of the court, I sat down and stretched with the team. Looking to my left, I continued to watch the seats in the arena fill up, and then I noticed her. The girl I saw in front of the arena—it was her.

I couldn't stop staring. What was she doing here? She worked for the athletic department? How haven't I noticed her before?

I continued to watch her make her way around the court until she found a seat right next to my coach. She said hello with a gentle smile to people who passed by. Her innocent face and radiant beauty hypnotized me. How was I supposed to play my best with her sitting right there?

I tried to turn my mind off. I tried my best to avoid looking at her, but my eyes continued to drift in that direction. We began to line up for the U.S. National Anthem, and that's when it happened. Our eyes locked, and everyone else in the arena disappeared. It was just the two of us in an empty arena. I was too mesmerized to look away. After she bent her head down for a few moments, I watched her slowly look back up. I smiled as our eyes met again hoping to get one in return.

Nothing.

Running back out onto the court after halftime, I looked up at the scoreboard and over to my coach. I played horribly during the first half. He actually asked me in the locker room if I knew how to play basketball. I was too distracted from glancing over at her, the way she looked intensely at what she was doing behind the computer and how she brushed her hair off to the right side of her face. I couldn't stop admiring everything about her. She, however, appeared to be trying her best to avoid looking at me.

The clock ran down again. I had one last chance to make this right. I couldn't miss any more rebounds or have the ball stolen from me. I needed to wake up. I needed to stop watching her and start playing a game she couldn't help but watch. So I did. I started making shot after shot and had no fouls. I was on fire. The Monmouth players couldn't keep up. Heck, my team couldn't even keep up with me.

At the buzzer, the adrenaline continued to rush through my body. I ran to my other teammates and pumped my fists in the air toward the crowd. Another win. Just as I was about to head into the locker room, a reporter came over to interview me.

"Wow, what a change of pace for you from the first half to the second! Can you elaborate to us on what happened?"

Taking a deep breath and wiping the sweat from my forehead, I looked over toward the girl and back at the reporter. Hands on my hips, I quickly had to think of a response.

"Well, we all have these days. My head just wasn't in the game during the first half. New semester, new classes, you know how that goes. But I owe a lot of my success to—" I tried to grab someone to help me escape from the interview, but the reporter continued, and no one was left. There was no way to get out of this now.

"Congratulations, by the way, on scoring your career high of fifty-three points! How do you do it? How do you make such a big mental switch?"

"You know, I'm going to tell you the same thing I told my kids at camp this summer. You have to want to win, and that has to be the only thing you want. If you for a second place your mind on something other than the game or playing your best, you'll lose it. Your time on the court is to be the best, play the best, work as a team, and bring that team to a win. You have the rest of the day to think about other things."

"Thanks for talking with us, Christian, and congratulations again!" The reporter closed when he noticed that my coach was waving me down to bring me into the locker room. Why couldn't he have waved me down sooner?

Once the last person entered the locker room, Coach Higgins started off with the same sentence after a win,

"Good job, guys. Another W is in the books. However…"

He continued to rip us apart for the mistakes we made, mostly my mistakes. He only mentioned once that I hit my career high. He was more focused on putting attention on how I needed to play more aggressively. Tomorrow morning we would hear all of this over again as we watched the game on film. I couldn't wait to watch how badly I played the first half.

The entire time he was ranting, all I could think about was getting back out into the arena and finding her.

As more time passed, I grew even more impatient. My legs were bouncing, my hands were clenched, and my eyes were glued on the door. I couldn't listen to him anymore, but I couldn't leave either.

I started to plan how I would make my escape as soon as he finished lecturing us. When he let us go, I did the exact opposite. My eyes remained glued to the door and my hands were now dripping with sweat. I was frozen. What would I even say to her?

"Still in shock about breaking the record? I would be too!" I heard the voice but chose to ignore it. Right now, I wasn't interested in carrying on a conversation with anyone except for one person.

Looking up at the clock, I noticed the time. Jumping up out of my seat and rushing toward the door, I didn't realize how much time I had spent debating if I should go talk to her or not. Now I may not even have a chance.

I didn't see her anywhere. The only people that were left in the arena were the cleaning crew and a few other workers. Disappointment filled me. The nerves disappeared since I had no reason to be nervous anymore. It wasn't until I turned around to head back toward the locker room that I noticed them.

Two girls were walking up the stairs toward the exit. I didn't even realize what I was doing until I had already yelled to get their attention.

"Excuse me," my voice carried throughout the empty arena. The girls stopped and turned around on instinct. Pointing to themselves, they wanted to confirm that I was indeed trying to get their attention. They seemed to be pretty shocked when I started running up the stairs toward them. I met the giggling girls halfway.

"Hi. Sorry if you were leaving, but I have a question. This may seem weird, so…well, I guess I'll just ask." Both of them continued to stare at me with surprised and confused looks on their faces. "Do either of you know what the girl's name was, the one who was sitting right next to the bench?" I pointed in the direction in which she was sitting earlier. "She was wearing a yellow sweater, long brown—"

Before I could finish, one of the girls interrupted me.

"Yes! I know her. Why do you ask?" She was inquisitive, and based on the tone of her voice, I could tell she not only knew her, but she was close to her.

"I have a question I need to ask her but never got a chance to tonight. Do you have her number by any chance? We have a class together, and it's about homework," I lied. I didn't want to seem like a creep.

The other girl didn't hesitate. "Ah, a class together. I see. Her name is Zoe, and here's her number," she said enthusiastically while reaching for her phone. It was obvious she knew I was lying.

"Thanks!" After entering her number in my phone, I almost tripped trying to back away down the stairs.

About to click onto a new message, I froze again. Just do it, I told myself. Just do it. I was so nervous, but why?

The pit in my stomach only grew deeper as soon as I pressed "send."

Who was this girl, and why was she doing this to me? Why did she make me feel this way?

{5}

Zoe

At the sound of the buzzer, I quickly picked up my things so I could make my escape. Although the game wasn't nearly as bad as I anticipated it would be, Christian caught me staring at him. My fast and abrupt exit allowed for me to leave the area without any confrontation from him.

Walking quickly up the stairs, I found my way to the concourse. As I weaved in and out of the crowd of fans leaving, all of their voices filled my head. I watched as the little girl next to me tugged at her father's hand and asked him if she was going to be able to get Christian Michaels' autograph. The teenage boys who passed me talked about how they wish they had skill like him. I was running, but I couldn't escape.

Finally exiting through the doors to the parking garage, an immediate pain shot through my chest after trying to take a deep breath. The temperature had dropped significantly, making it even harder for me to breathe.

In the car, I blasted the heat and turned the volume up. Keith Urban came on, and a smile of relief appeared on my face. Singing loudly, I jammed out to the sweet sound of victory. I was able to get myself out of what could have been another embarrassing scenario. The next song had just started when my phone interrupted and began to ring. It was Emily.

"Hey. Is everything okay?" I was still humming the chorus of the last song.

"Yeah, everything's great! Home yet?"

"No, not yet. I just left. My car took a while to defrost and the roads are awful!" I carefully pressed on the brakes, afraid that my car would catch the slick roads and slide.

"Should have just started your car and waited in the arena with us!"

"I didn't think it was going to take this long. I didn't know we were supposed to get this much snow, either."

"Well, still, you should have. Want to know why?"

"Why?" I knew she was up to something.

"Christian came up to me and asked for your number."

"You're real funny. I am so glad he didn't talk to me. I was so nervous at the table. Glad I avoided that one! Although—"

"I'm serious," Emily interrupted my sentence.

"What do you mean?" That smile on my face disappeared, and my nerves caught back up to me. Emily was an awful liar, and I could hear it in her voice that she was telling the truth.

"Like I said, he came up to me right after you left, and—"

"You're joking. No, he didn't." I panicked.

"Yes, he did, and he asked for your number! Will you just listen? Jeez!"

"Please don't tell me you gave it to him! Emily, ugh, I told you I wasn't interested. You're joking." I was frozen at the steering wheel.

"Zoe, do you realize how lucky you are? If I could have pretended to be you, I would have. It's Christian Michaels!"

"Relax. He probably won't even text me." The snow continued to hit my windshield even heavier than before.

"Seriously? He's going to text you. He isn't just going to ask a random girl for your number then not text you."

"I just don't understand. Why is he even interested? What does he want from me?"

"Well, if I were you, I wouldn't be complaining! This is what you wanted, right?"

"Yeah, well…I mean…I don't know. I'm almost home, though," I lied to end the conversation. Cars behind me beeped loudly when the light turned green and my foot remained on the brake. Right now getting home safe was more of a priority than Christian texting me. "I'll let you know if he texts me, okay?"

"He will." Emily spoke confidently. "Tell Gabe I said hi and that I'll come see him soon. Get some rest tonight."

"Okay, I will. Thank you. The snow is pretty bad, so drive safe!"

Hanging up the phone, I threw it into my purse on the passenger's seat. Barely able to see through the windows, my slight panic had now turned into a full blown panic attack. Concentrating on the roads became tough when I couldn't stop thinking about if he was going to text me. What would I even say?

*

I could hardly pull into my driveway with the snow that had accumulated on the ground. Opening the front door to the house, I hit my boots against the steps to knock all of the snow off. My body stung as I entered into my warm house. I was frozen. Quietly walking up the stairs, I stood outside of Gabe's room and listened as he spoke out loud.

At first it sounded like he was in the middle of a conversation with Janice, our neighbor who helps us out, but I soon realized he was praying. Listening closely, I leaned against the wall and slowly sank to the floor. I've never met a more positive and joyous young boy than him. His attitude was probably one of the only things that kept him strong for being so weak. Tears were building up in the corner of my eye.

"…for another day, and for my sister, especially my sister. But I don't think she's happy. I try to make her laugh, but I think she fakes it sometimes. Can you please tell her that I'm okay? Thanks, God. I appreciate it." I sneezed and he stopped speaking.

"Zoe? Is that you? Are you home?"

Quietly jumping to my feet and wiping the tears away, I crept around the corner. "Hey! Just got home! How was your night?"

"I saw you on TV! I didn't know you sat on the court," he yelled excitedly and greeted me with a hug.

"They asked me to do something different today. Great game, huh?"

"Yeah, Michaels played amazing! When I'm feeling better can I meet him? He's so good. I have to go see him this year. It's his last year. Can I go to a game? Please? Please? Pretty please?"

"Calm down there, buddy!" I laughed, and at the same time I felt sick. I had to lie. He was right. The season was almost over, and I didn't see that there was any way he would be well enough to go. "I promise that if you get better, I will take you to go see him play." I had to give him some hope.

Gabe was wearing his number 7 shirt, Christian Michaels' number, and he covered himself with his new Siena basketball blanket. He idolized him and the team, which was primarily the reason why I didn't want to get to know him. I didn't want him to break not only my heart, but Gabe's. His heart was much more fragile than mine.

I closed the door behind me and noticed that there was a light on in what used to be my parents' bedroom. Gabe must have gone in there. The door creaked open when I slightly touched it with the ball of my foot. Grabbing onto the doorknob, I tried to quietly close it. Sitting down on the bed, I looked around at everything that remained untouched. Life has become too busy and stressful to begin thinking about packing up the things my mother left behind. My eyes glanced over toward the last picture we had with her from Gabe's fifth birthday party. I shook my head in anger and shut off the light.

I headed down the stairs so I could finally send Janice home. She had been cleaning the dishes and walking through the house. I noticed she must have done a full house cleaning for me today. She did so much for us even though she didn't have to. She took us in as if we were her own children. It started to anger me. How could someone be so selfless and sacrifice everything for someone else's' children when our own mother couldn't even do that?

"I can finish those later." I placed a plate from Gabe's room next to the sink.

"It's okay! Don't worry about it. Do you want me to make you something to eat? I'm sure you have to be starving. You've had a long day!" Janice turned the water off and dried off her hands.

"No, really, you don't have to! I'll grab something."

"I made homemade meatballs and pasta. Let me heat up some for you." She headed straight toward the fridge.

"My favorite? Thank you!" I sat down at the kitchen table.

"I figured I would surprise you after the week you've had."

Her words opened up the emotions I've been trying to hide over the last twenty-four hours. My vision was clouded through the tears, and I started to weep.

"Oh, honey, what's wrong?" Janice pulled out the chair next to me and embraced me in her arms.

"I just don't know how I can repay you for everything you do for us."

"You don't have to! I already told you that. I'm always here for you anytime you need me. You and your brother are like my children." She handed me a tissue to wipe the tears away from my eyes.

"That's just it. We aren't even your children. We're not even family, and you love us like we are. No offense, but how can you do that and our own mother couldn't?" I thought about the picture in her room and how different our lives were back then.

"I know it's hard to understand, Zoe. We may never understand what was going through your mother's head when she left you two, but you know how much she loved the both of you."

"If she loved us she wouldn't have left us."

"She left the day after Gabe was diagnosed with cancer. After going through your father's death, I'm not sure she was ready to deal with seeing her child suffer. Now, I'm not making any excuses for her, but—"

"I know, I know. She didn't even grieve Dad's death well. I think it would have been harder for me if I had to take care of her and Gabe. I just wish…and I hate saying this, but I wish she wasn't so selfish and got herself help before just taking the easy route and leaving us behind to fend for ourselves."

"You're not alone. You both have me, and you know that I'll never leave either of you in the dark." Janice smiled and rubbed my back.

"Do you remember how long it took for Gabe to accept your help?" I chuckled a little bit.

"He did not like me. He thought I was some mean old lady coming to punish him."

"He had quite the personality for a five year old, didn't he?"

"He locked his room and wouldn't let me in the second day you left me with him."

We both laughed. Thinking back, it was a hard adjustment for such a little kid, but now I can't imagine our lives without Janice.

After eating her delicious meatballs, I sent Janice on her way home. She only lived down the road, but I felt bad for making her stay out late often.

I had completely forgotten about my phone call with Emily earlier until I grabbed my phone off of the charger and noticed the unknown number on my screen.

I turned off all of the lights in the house and locked the doors, before heading up to my room. I set my phone down on the nightstand next to me. After a half hour of tossing and turning, I couldn't put my mind to rest unless I read the message. I slid my finger to the right and read the words that popped up on my screen.

{6}

Christian

I reached for my phone to check the time—6:45 a.m. Even on my days off, I couldn't seem to sleep in. My body was programmed to wake up before the sun rose. Lying in bed I could try and force myself to fall back to sleep, but I knew by now that I wouldn't have any luck. My mind was in a fog. These days I couldn't seem to find clarity.

I went for a light jog once I was able to get out of bed. I thought it might help clear my mind, but I couldn't even make it halfway across campus without having to stop and catch my breath. The air was so cold that it was tough to breathe. I could barely feel my fingers inside my insulated gloves. By the time I made it to the dining hall, my eyelashes appeared to be frozen like icicles, and it hurt to bend my fingers. Walking inside, I grabbed a hot cup of coffee and nearly burned my frozen lips while taking a sip.

After my hands finally were relieved of the numbness, I had to force myself to enter back outside into the cold. The run back seemed much farther than it actually was. I couldn't wait to jump into a hot shower. I glided across campus, quickly testing my speed against the cold wind. I ran into my house and straight to the bathroom and stripped my body of my clothes.

Standing underneath the scorching hot water, I prolonged reaching for the shampoo. The burning sensation against my frozen skin felt more desirable than it should.

"Hey, Chris! Who's Zoe?" Matthew shouted from the room beside me. My phone must have gone off or—because he can't mind his own business—he had to check it. It didn't surprise me, which is why I changed my passcode again last night. He was one of those people who had to know everything.

I turned off the water and quickly jumped out of the shower. While running out the door to grab my phone, I almost forgot to wrap a towel around myself. My body slammed against my bedroom door when I tried to push it open.

"Tell me who she is and I'll let you in."

"She's a girl in a class I'm working on a project with—jeez, open the door. I'm getting water all over the hallway."

"I call bullshit. If she was, you would have yelled that from the shower."

I paused. By now I should have known he was going to do this. I never learned my lesson.

"So? I'm waiting."

"If you let me in, I'll tell you."

I waited. He still refused to open the door. At twenty-one years old, he still acted like a child.

"Okay, you win. I ran into her the other day and spilled her coffee. Then I saw her at the basketball game and asked her friend for her number," I replied, sighing.

"You what?" He opened the door, handing me the phone with an expression of surprise on his face.

"Yeah. It's not a big deal, okay?" I grabbed my phone and headed toward my bed.

"Not a big deal? You never ask some random girl for someone else's number."

"So?" I was nervous to see what she had said. I probably shouldn't have flat out asked her on a date, but once I had already hit send, it was too late to take it back. I wasn't thinking clearly. Confused as to why I have never noticed her before, I acted before I thought. I didn't want to miss another chance. Something about this girl made me worry.

"She hot?" Matthew sat on his desk still anxiously waiting for more details.

"No. She's beautiful."

"When will I get to meet her? This sounds serious."

Matthew's words went in one ear and out the other. I could hear him talking faintly. My thoughts echoed loudly in my head. Looking at the wall, my mind drifted and I pictured her sitting in front of me at the game. I fantasized what it would be like to spend time with her. I wondered what would have happened if I had just left the locker room when I had the chance. Would I have caught her before she left? Would I have asked her out then or just asked for her number? I was captivated by her beauty. Something then hit me in the back of the head.

"Hello. Earth to Chris. Are you going to be bringing her back to the room anytime soon? I want to see this chick."

"No, probably not for a while." Which was true. That wasn't my intention with Zoe. She appeared to be different. I wanted to get to know her on the inside. For some reason, when I thought of Zoe, I had a burning desire for something more, something real.

"Oh, so you're going to avoid introducing us, and you're going to go to her place, huh?"

"No, that's not what I'm saying at all. I asked her to go to dinner with me. I want to take her out on an actual date."

"Shut up. Seriously? You're ready to date again?"

"Well, no—I mean, I can be. I wasn't planning for this to happen, but I can't stop thinking about her, and I want to get to know her. I'm not saying it'll be anything serious. I don't know if I want a girlfriend, and I don't even really know her. I'm just going with my gut on this one, and my gut is telling me she's different in a good way. My gut tells me I need to get to know her and that something on the more serious side is maybe what I need."

Matthew stared at me with a blank look on his face. "What more could you possibly need? How would a girl change that?"

"I can't really explain." I couldn't seem to put my thoughts into words.

"Well, we're young and in school. We should have fun."

"You can still have fun. All I'm saying is, personally, this is maybe what I need."

"You could have anything or any girl you want in this school. I don't think you should be trying so hard for this one girl. You've never had to take a girl on a date before to get her to like you. Why change your ways now?"

I left the room. Matt and I were at very different places in our lives, and he didn't seem to understand what I was saying. I'm not even sure I am understanding what I am feeling or why this one girl is making me want to be a better man, but she is.

I threw on a pair of sweats over my boxers and sat in my bed. I stared down at my phone, afraid to see what Zoe had said.

What if she says no?

This was nerve wracking. I'm twenty-two years old, and I've never asked a girl out on a date before. Here I am a senior in college, a guy who always has girls fawning all over him, and I've never asked a girl out. Matt's words haunted me too. What if I come across as a douchebag to her? What if I'm not good enough?

What if she says yes?

I didn't have a plan. I would need to find somewhere nice to take her. Around here there were only a few options. It was nothing like the city. I would want the night to be perfect.

Should I get her flowers? Should I pick her up? I thought to myself, making a mental note of everything I should be prepared for. I've never needed to impress a girl before. This was new for me. I couldn't screw it up.

Opening the text, I stared at the screen and locked my phone. I stared at the black screen and saw the reflection of what appeared to be a smile on my face.

"'I would love to,'" I whispered her response to myself quietly.

{7}

Zoe

"Hi, honey. How was class today?" Janice picked up the phone on the first ring.

"Oh, it was okay. I'm actually calling to see if you would be able to stay later tonight. I have this…thing."

"Sure, don't worry about it. What time should I tell Gabe you will be home?"

I looked around at my surroundings and on the path ahead to see if anyone was around. I was headed toward the library to get some homework done. All I needed was for someone to overhear my conversation and spread it around campus.

"Here's the thing. I actually don't know. I'm, um, sort of going on a date tonight. Can you do me a favor and keep this between us? I don't want Gabe to know."

"A date?" Janice exclaimed loudly. I pulled the phone away from my ear.

"Shh. I don't want Gabe to hear you!"

"He won't. He's taking a nap right now. Oh honey, I'm so happy for you!" I could hear it in her voice that she was smiling on the other end of the line. She always wanted the best for me and has wanted me to date for a while now.

"Yeah, I'm still not sure about it. There's still time to back out. I don't know. Maybe I won't go."

"Is he nice?"

"I'm not sure. I don't know that much about him."

"Do you in your heart truly want to go tonight?"

I pondered on her question for a while. Christian Michaels asking me out on a date has been a fantasy of mine that I never thought would become real.

"Yeah, I guess. I just—"

Janice interrupted, "Don't even think about it. Just go! Have a good time. I can't wait to hear all about it. I'm sure it will go smoothly. Take your time coming home."

"Thanks, Janice. I don't know what I would do without you."

"No need to thank me! Plus, think about how happy your parents would be for you."

I stopped in the middle of the walkway and took a deep breath.

"You're right." I smiled. "They always wanted the best for me."

"They did, as all parents should for their children. I remember your mom used to tell me about those heels she bought you as a little girl because you wanted to look nice for a date."

I laughed while looking down at my feet and then realized I had nothing to wear for tonight. All of my sadness of wishing both of my parents were here to hear about my first date slid right out the window. What was I going to wear?

"I did love those! But thanks again, Janice. I should go. I'm about to go into the library."

"Have a good time! I cannot wait to hear all about it. And remember, all you have to do is be yourself."

Hanging up the phone, I quickly dialed Emily's number.

"Emily, I need your help."

*

After classes, I didn't even go home. Emily said she would help me get ready. She had a knack for fashion and getting ready at her dorm room made it even easier for Gabe to avoid seeing me all dressed up. He would wonder where I was going and start to ask questions. I wouldn't be able to lie to his face.

My nerves were starting to kick in. I didn't know where Christian was taking me; the only detail he gave me was to be ready by seven. I couldn't stop thinking about what tonight might be like. The only dates I ever went on in high school were to the movies, and I'm pretty sure those don't even count. Everything was completely different now. We were older, standards were higher, more was expected, and I had more responsibilities—a lot more than most people my age.

Emily lived in the suites in one of the underclassmen dorms. As a junior, she and her suitemates didn't have a high enough lottery number to get into the townhouses. I've never had the chance to live on campus. There have been a few weekends where I stayed with Emily and tried to pretend I knew what campus life was like. I envied Emily for that. It wasn't an option for me. It never was.

When I arrived at her room, the door was propped open. Knocking slightly, I could hear her yell for me to come in. I walked in and I took a look around. Her entire side of the room had outfits laid out accordingly. The curling iron was on, and make-up was spread out across her desk.

"Are you ready to get beautiful? I mean, you already are, but you know what I mean." Emily could hardly talk. I could tell she was beaming with excitement. She was more thrilled about this than I was. Like me, she also thought Christian was incredibly gorgeous. Neither of us ever thought one of us would have the chance.

"I guess so. It's so cold out, though. I don't know what I should wear." I looked around at some of the options she had laid out.

"You are such a baby when it comes to the cold weather!"

"I can't help it! I swear I belong in the south."

"Don't we all? How do you want your hair? It's so long. I can do curls. I can put it up? It's completely up to you."

"Can I figure out what I'm wearing first? Then I'll decide on my hair."

"Sure. I have a few things out, and, um, please don't kill me." She paused.

"A few things? It looks like you could fill an entire closet with all of these clothes! But, um, what did you do?"

"I may have sort of told my roommate about your date. But before you say anything, I really liked this one outfit of hers, and I knew she wouldn't let me borrow it unless I told her what it was for." Emily was talking a mile a minute to get all the words out before I could interrupt her.

I had a feeling this might happen because if Emily gets really excited about something, she had to tell everyone about it. It wasn't even on purpose; she just couldn't help it.

"What outfit?" I said back with a slight attitude, and I placed my hands on my hips.

Walking toward the far corner of the room, Emily stood with her back to me and picked up a dress from her bed. Turning around she held it up to the light.

"Tell me this isn't perfect." She grinned and watched for me to make a reaction.

She was right. The dress was perfect. It was three-quarter sleeved, which would prevent me from getting too cold. The top layer was lace patterned with a solid green underneath, which made it classy but also casual.

"It would go great with your green eyes, and I have black tights and tall boots that would match perfectly!" Her eyes were lit up with excitement. Grabbing it from her hands, I placed it down on the bed beside me and started to undress. Slipping it on, I stared at myself in the full body mirror. Emily sat there biting her lip, impatiently waiting to hear what I thought of the dress.

"I think this might be it. I love it!"

"Knew you would!" She jumped off of the bed and ran over to

the bathroom. "Now the next question. What are we doing with your hair? Have you thought about it yet?" She asked.

"Um, down? Maybe long curls? What do you think?"

"Knew you would say that! I was thinking the same thing when I saw this dress. I already have my curling iron and wand turned on. You have to be ready by six forty-five-ish, right?"

"Maybe a little earlier so I'm not rushing. He said to be ready by seven."

"Okay, well, that is manageable. Where do you think he is taking you?"

"No idea, to be honest." I wondered.

"Maybe he's taking you to Saratoga or to an expensive restaurant. I mean, he can afford it."

"That would be nice, but I'm not sure. I'm trying not to think too much about it. I don't want to get my hopes up and be disappointed, you know? I mean, I know this probably won't work out anyway."

"How do you know that?"

"I mean, think about it, Emily. We won't have anything to talk about. He's from a rich family with a perfect life. Mine's far from perfect, and I'm far from rich."

"Yeah, but you never know. Maybe you have more in common than you think. You don't know unless you try. Give yourself a little more credit. He's going to fall in love with you."

"Let's slow it down."

Emily set the curling iron down for a moment. "Listen. I know you are going into this pessimistically, but you have to look at the bright side of things. What if this works out? What if you enjoy yourself? You could have an amazing time, and he could end up being the perfect guy. But you won't know if you go into this thinking negatively. You won't open yourself up to these opportunities because you're going to try and find something that will go wrong. So try to think positively about this." Everything she was saying was true.

"I know, I know, you're right. But all I'm saying is that I don't think it will go well, and I don't think I can date anyone right now, especially because of Gabe."

"Zoe, oh Zoe, Gabe knows how much you care about him. Your dad wouldn't want you to put your life on hold. You do so much for your brother already, and I'm sure if you were to date someone, Gabe would be really happy for you. Maybe this is what you need in your life anyway!"

"And that's just it, I can't start dating someone and introduce them to Gabe. He would be so upset if it didn't work out. Especially since it's Christian!"

"There you go thinking negative again. Who says it won't work out? You never know! Maybe he's the miracle you both need."

Emily was an overly optimistic person, but I can't even deny that what she's saying is true. Because she saw things with a positive eye, she always seemed to know exactly what I needed in my life to brighten up my days. Maybe she was right. Maybe Christian will end up being the light I need.

"I didn't tell Gabe about my date. I don't want him knowing anything unless it gets more serious. And that's a big if! It's just one date, Emily. Just one. Let's not make more out of this than what it actually is."

"And one turns into two, and two into three, and before you know it I'll be the maid of honor at—"

"Stop!" I laughed. Emily was finishing my hair and nearly burned my back when she dropped the wand.

My hair was almost done. I loved it. Emily should have gone to school for cosmetology. I could never get my hair to look this good when I curled it myself, which was almost never. I never had any time to spend a lot of time on my hair. I looked down at my watch. It was six fifteen. I panicked, thinking that I wouldn't be ready in time since my make-up still wasn't done. My phone began to ring.

"Hello?" I answered it quickly before seeing who was even calling.

"Zoe, when will you be home?" It was Gabe. The sound of his voice worried me, and I second-guessed if I should go or not.

"Not until later buddy. Everything okay? How's your day?"

"Yeah, everything's great! Janice made me cookies, and we are going to watch a movie tonight."

"Oh, that's good! Make sure you thank her before you go to sleep! If you start to not feel well, stop eating the cookies."

"She told me you're going somewhere special tonight, so I just wanted to call and tell you to have a great time." Those words broke my heart. He truly meant it. I wish I could tell him where I was headed. He sounded excited for me even though he had no idea what I was doing. A smile faintly appeared on my face.

"Aw, thanks, bud. I'm sure I will! Don't give Janice too much trouble, okay?"

"Okay! Goodnight, Zoe. Love you!"

"Love you too, buddy."

"Are you okay?" Emily asked as she stared at me through the mirror.

"Yeah, it was Gabe."

"I could tell. Is everything okay?"

"Yeah, he just wanted to tell me to have a good time."

"Aw, see! I told you. Everything is going to be okay! Just relax. Gabe is fine and you are going to have a great night!"

"I sure hope so," I replied with doubt.

*

Seven o'clock came too quickly. I wasn't ready for this. But where was Christian? It was now ten minutes after, and I was standing here thinking of the endless possibilities of how this could go wrong, starting with being ditched. Hopefully he was just late and not standing me up. Despite my request, Emily stood beside me to wait.

"I don't think he's coming." I sighed.

"He's just running late. Give it a few more minutes."

"It's already been ten! Who is ten minutes late to pick up their date, on their first date?"

"Relax, relax. Oh wait, isn't that him?" Emily yelled with excitement in her voice.

A black BMW pulled up into the horseshoe in front of the building. Emily and I couldn't see who it was because of the dark tinted windows. It had to be him. What other college student drives a brand new BMW?

The car shut off, and the driver's door opened. Through the darkness I watched a tall and very attractive guy walk around to the passenger's side of the car. Leaning up against the door, the guy reached in his pocket and pulled his phone out. Seconds later my phone went off.

{8}

Christian

I leaned against the passenger's side door, watching her walk with grace as she headed toward me. I knew by now that I was smiling like an idiot.

"You look beautiful." I watched a small smile appear on her face as she approached.

"Thank you." She looked at me with an innocence in her eyes that drove me wild.

"Sorry I'm late." I held the door open for her she slowly got in the car. "I wanted to make sure the car was warm enough since it's gotten colder out. I hope I didn't worry you."

"That's okay. You didn't at all."

"Are you warm enough? I can turn the heat up more."

"No, this is perfect."

You're right. This is perfect, I thought to myself as I looked over, noticing how beautiful she looked even in the darkness.

*

The table I had reserved for us was placed toward the back in a corner, which ensured us a little more privacy. Three candles were lit in the center, and the lights were dim, making the setting a bit more romantic. Staring at the menu, I didn't know what to say to her. Maybe this was a little bit too much pressure for a first date. Maybe I should have taken her for ice cream instead.

I picked up my menu and pretended to read over it. I couldn't think of a way to start a conversation. My eyes peered over the top of the menu. She had her menu placed out in front of her, and she moved around in her seat.

I cleared my throat and reached to take a sip of water. We made eye contact this time. I continued to drink until I thought of something to say that could end the awkward silence. I placed my half empty glass down on the table.

"So what do you do at the basketball games?"

"I just do promotions stuff. You know, throwing t-shirts, getting chants going, all that good stuff." Her eyes dropped down to the menu again.

"Oh, that's cool. What were you doing at the last game when you were sitting at the scorer's table?"

"I had to administer the social media pages. You played really incredible that game!"

"Thank you. I'm surprised I was able to play that well, but I haven't had a bad game yet. It's really starting to hit me that the season's almost over, though."

"Yeah, I bet that can't be easy for you." She looked around the restaurant and back down at her menu again. Avoiding eye contact with me seemed to be a skill of hers. I could sense her frustration. I don't think she wanted to talk about basketball.

"So are you from around here?"

"Yeah, I've lived here my entire life. I didn't really have a choice but to go to college around here. Not that Siena isn't great, but I would have liked to have some options."

"Oh. Why's that?"

"Family stuff. So what are you going to get?" The tone in her voice quickly changed, and she seemed sad, leaving me with the impression that I shouldn't bring it up again. At least not tonight. Luckily the waitress came over and interrupted us.

Looking up, I made eye contact with her, and her hands started to shake when she grabbed her pen from her pocket. I speculated it was because she knew who I was. She had a familiar face, but I don't think that I know her.

Wait. Shit. I know exactly who she is, I thought to myself, trying to keep my head down and avoid eye contact.

"Hello, my name is Katha, and I'll be your waitress for tonight. Can I get you something to drink?" she said. I could tell that she wasn't even looking at me since her voice projected more toward Zoe.

"I'll just have a water with a lemon."

"And for you, Chris?" She said in an underlying bitchy tone.

"I'll do the same." Even though I wanted to get a beer, I wasn't sure how Zoe would feel about that. As it was, having Katha as our waitress tonight completely threw me for a loop. Hopefully this wouldn't screw up anything.

"You know her?" Zoe questioned when she walked away.

"Sort of. She's one of the girls I previously had a thing with."

Shit, why do I always have to tell the truth? It just comes out without warning. I should really start thinking before I speak.

"Oh, one of the girls?" She didn't look happy, but she also appeared to be interested. I couldn't tell if she was being sarcastic or serious.

"Yeah, after Lacey and I broke up I went through this phase."

"Oh, I see." She wasn't amused.

"It's over with now though; hence I'm out with you."

Hopefully she doesn't take that the wrong way. I immediately regretted saying that.

"Well, I would hope so. Did you go out with her too?" She asked nodding her head over toward another waitress who was eyeing me.

"No, no. I promise I'm not like that."

There was an awkward silence. I no longer knew what to say. Anything I was saying wasn't helping me at all.

"If you don't mind me asking, why me?" Zoe broke the silence.

"What do you mean?"

"Why did you ask me out tonight?"

"I want to get to know you." I wasn't expecting her to ask such a question. It caught me off guard.

"You do?"

"Yeah. You seem surprised?"

"I am. Guys like you don't usually ask me out."

"Guys like me?" What is that supposed to mean?

"Yeah, you know, the popular and attractive jocks that everyone wants to date."

"So you think I'm attractive?" I smiled confidently and my nerves disappeared a little.

"You know what I mean. I'm just surprised, that's all." Zoe blushed.

Katha was headed back over toward us. I didn't even know what to order for dinner. I've hardly looked at the menu, and it was quite extensive. Plus, right across from me at the table was the most beautiful girl I've ever seen.

The green dress she wore brought out the emerald in her eyes. Much of her flawless skin was revealed when she pulled her dark brown hair over her right shoulder. From where I was sitting, I could see she had a tattoo on the side of her neck going down the back of her shoulder. Diamond earrings in her ears, she had a total of five piercings, one of which included a bar through the top of her ear, giving her a more edgy look.

I couldn't take my eyes off of her.

*

The car ride back to Siena was silent. Arriving on campus, I drove her to her car. I stared out the front windshield trying to think of how I could prolong the night. All I wanted to do was know more about her.

"I hope you had a great time. If it's okay, I'd like to take you out again soon?" I asked her nervously while fiddling with the keys in my hand. I could hardly look her in the eye while speaking. The words slowly found their way out of my mouth.

"Honestly, I didn't know what to expect out of tonight. It was the first date I've been on in a while."

"Same for me."

"What? I don't believe that. I mean, you with all your girls—you don't need to lie to make me feel better," she replied sarcastically.

"I'm not lying. I'm dead serious. Lacey and I didn't even go out on dates."

"Seriously? Why not?"

"I guess it didn't seem like much of a relationship to me. I just did whatever she said and did my own thing when I wasn't with her. Great boyfriend, I know."

"I don't know what you want out of this." Quickly the conversation became more serious.

"Honestly, I don't either. All I know is I want to see you again and I want to learn everything there is to know about you, Zoe." The truth came out of my mouth before I could stop it.

"Why? And again, why me? You could have any girl in this school if you wanted to."

"But I asked you out, not any of the other girls. I asked you. Ever since you ran into me—"

"You mean you ran into me," Zoe replied fiercely. She wasn't making this easy.

"But right then, I couldn't stop thinking about you and how I've never seen you before."

Zoe took what seemed to be a long minute before responding.

"I'm extremely busy, and I have a lot going on. I have to go. So thanks for dinner. Goodnight."

She unbuckled her seatbelt, got out of the car, and shut the door without even looking back. I don't know what it was that I said to make her mad.

What was I doing wrong?

I sat here questioning myself more than I ever have before. Putting my keys back into the ignition, I turned the car on and headed back toward my townhouse.

The rain poured down heavily on my windshield, obstructing my vision. Driving around aimlessly, I continued to fail miserably at finding a parking spot close to my building. Bad luck seemed to be following me around tonight, especially on my date with Zoe—the date I just completely blew for myself.

{9}

Zoe

Livid was a better word than disappointed to describe how I felt about last night. How could I be disappointed if I wasn't expecting anything? But was I really not expecting anything, or was I just trying to convince myself that I wasn't? I was more mad at the fact I was putting myself through this, though. Christian was exactly who I thought he was, the person I didn't want him to be. Right from the beginning I had a feeling it wouldn't go well. I tried not to think about it all day, but I couldn't stop.

I will admit that at the start of the night I convinced myself that maybe it wouldn't be so bad. He shocked me by opening the car door for me, followed by pulling the seat out at the restaurant. Acting like a gentleman, he looked like one too. Dressed in a shirt and tie, it was one of the first times I've ever seen him dressed nice since he was always wearing basketball apparel.

Lost in thought, I almost missed Emily's phone call. She was probably checking in on me to make sure I wasn't ditching the game today. The game. I really didn't want to go and face him after I made my exit from his car.

As soon as I picked up, she didn't even give me the chance to have the first word.

"Oh, good! You're alive. I was wondering since I have yet to hear from you about your date last night!" She spoke energetically.

"Well, I'm pretty sure that was the first and last time we will go out."

"Why? Please don't tell me you did anything stupid or ruined it because you weren't open to it. You know what? Just tell me later. Want to grab a drink before the game?"

"That sounds good. What time should we meet?"

"Well, we have to be there by five. The game's at six today. I was thinking maybe three?"

"Perfect. I'll see you then."

Having a drink before the game may calm me down before walking into the arena. I wasn't prepared to see Christian. I didn't want to get to know him anymore. Last night probably could have gone better if I had been more positive about it. A part of me really wanted this, but I knew that it wasn't realistic. What would be the point?

*

"Okay, fine. I won't tell you anymore." I sat there angrily staring at Emily.

"Okay, okay, I'm sorry. Go on," Emily apologized. As much as she wanted me to have a boyfriend, she also loved to mock my love life.

"All he did was talk about himself. Once basketball was brought up, forget it. Want to know what pissed me off the most? He brought up how he's never seen me before. We had a class together for an entire semester! The class only had twenty kids in it. I've passed him so many times on campus before. So how hasn't he seen me? How didn't recognize me?"

"Oh my God, I would be pissed too. Did he really say that?" Emily put her glass down.

"Yes! He really he did."

46

"Well, I think you should give the guy another chance. You might be overreacting just a tad. I don't remember half of the people I've had classes with. Has he texted you yet today?" I could tell she was trying to rationalize with me since I was clearly just making up excuses.

"Another chance? Why? So I will get hurt? I don't think he's my type. But to answer your question, yeah, he did. But I didn't respond, and I don't plan on it." I sulked in my seat and drowned my throat with a huge gulp of beer.

"Zoe, Zoe, Zoe." Emily stared at me.

"What?" I put my glass down and stared back.

"You don't know if he's good for you yet. You haven't really given him a chance. I think you should go for it. I think this will be a good thing. You need a guy in your life."

"No."

Emily looked did a quick turn around in her seat. "But it's been years since you've had sex."

"What the hell? Say it loud enough so the whole bar can hear it."

"What? It's true! You haven't since freshman year, and that was, like, drunk sex."

"I haven't wanted to. I don't want a guy in my life, and I certainly don't need sex to be happy."

"Well, it doesn't hurt to just have casual sex every once in a while," Emily suggested.

"I really don't think that this is going to work out. I have the entire universe voting against me. I don't know. I really don't. What about Gabe?"

"Gabe will be fine! You know how he looks up to him. Just imagine how happy he will be when you tell him! Imagine his reaction when he meets him."

"Which is exactly why I can't if it doesn't work out."

"You don't know it won't yet. Can I see the text he sent you?"

"Why?"

"Just let me see it," Emily demanded.

I opened up the text and looked at it once more before handing it to her.

"Okay. Done." She responded shortly after looking at my phone. I was a little bit tipsy, and I didn't think before I handed it to her.

"What's done? What! No, you didn't!" I shrieked louder than expected. She slid my phone across the table, and I read the words on the screen. She'd replied to Christian's text for me.

"Why did you do that?"

"You needed a little push. Trust me; this is going to work. You need to at least try."

The bartender came over to see if we needed a refill. I wanted one, but I had to go to the game sober enough to work.

Staring at the screen, I continued to read what Emily had typed out. The simple message of "Good luck at your game today" freaked me out. The bubble at the bottom left corner popped up. He was responding.

"He's typing back already!"

"See! I told you to listen to me! Look how excited you just got!"

I flipped my phone over onto its front side, and the two of us stared at it without blinking.

"Just read it. If you won't, I will." Emily went to reach for my phone, but I snatched it quickly.

"Thanks! Wanna go out after the game?" It took me a few moments to continue reading all of the words to her.

"Yay! You have to say yes!" Emily yelled.

"You really think so? Even though the first date went horrible?"

"How much worse could it really get? Just give him another chance."

"Yeah, I could do that." I read my text to Emily as I typed back.

"See? How hard was that?"

"'Great. I have a surprise for you.'" I looked up at Emily, and we both stared at one another, then I looked back down at the text again.

What could the surprise be? How could he already have a surprise for me?

"How am I going to explain this to Gabe?" I panicked.

"Oh. you'll think of something! Just tell him you have to work on school stuff in the library after the game."

"I hate lying to him. I feel like I never have time to hang out with him anymore. He's going to start to wonder if I keep ditching him. You know how smart he is."

"Well," Emily said while looking at her phone, "we have one hour until game time. How much more excited are you now for what this night is going to bring?"

"I'm not. I'm not excited at all." The truth was that I was probably glowing with excitement, and she could see it all over my face.

Maybe I was wrong. Maybe this could be a good thing. Maybe I'd just need to open myself up to these opportunities. But maybe I'd be right and this wouldn't work out. I was so torn between what to do and how I should act. My heart was telling me to go for it, but my head was saying it wouldn't be a good idea. Right now I wondered what my parents would say if I asked them for their advice. In times like these I missed them more than usual, and I envied my friends who took advantage of having their parents around.

What do I do? How do I know what to do?

{10}

Gabe

"Janice! Jan! Janny!"

Rushing into my room, she was almost out of breath.

"What's wrong? Is everything okay?"

"Yeah, everything's great!"

"Damn it, Gabe! I told you to stop doing that to me. You know what that can do to me at my age. I could have a heart attack. Then who would take care of you when Zoe isn't here?"

"I'm sorry. I really am. But I have a secret to tell you."

"What's that?"

"Come here. I can't tell you unless I whisper it."

She leaned in closer, and I told her the secret into her ears.

By the look on her face as she backed away, I know Zoe probably already called her. Zoe probably told her where she was going, though. I don't know why she can't just tell me. I mean, I am her brother. She told me I was her best friend. Don't best friends tell each other these things?

"So, what do you think? Am I right?"

"I don't know anything." Janice backed away.

"She's going somewhere and told me she won't be home until late. She has to be with a boy."

"If she wants you to know, she will tell you."

"She's keeping secrets from me, and I don't like it!"

"She's your older sister. Older sisters always keep secrets from their little brothers. I did from mine."

"But not Zoe. She doesn't do that. Can you hand me the walkie from over there? It's almost game time!"

"What do you say? How do you ask?"

"Oh! Please, can I have the walkie talkie?"

"There's your manners! I thought you had lost them somewhere!"

She grabbed it and put it in my hand, turning it on for me, but just when I thought she was going to leave my room she sat down on my bed beside me.

"Can I give you some advice?"

"When don't you, Jan?"

"My name is Janice. Now, Gabriel—"

"My name is Gabe."

"Oh, you are just something else, aren't you? Well, sometimes Zoe doesn't tell you things for your own good. She is your sister. She does a lot for you. If she asks you not to call her, you need to obey that. You understand that? Did she ask you not to call her?"

She stared down at my phone questioning me.

"Aw, come on. I just want to see where she is and who she is with."

Her hand reached out to grab it.

"Do I have to take away the phone again?"

"No..." I hesitated.

"Good."

We used the walkie-talkies to communicate so I didn't have to yell to her. She hated using it. She says she's too old for a phone like I have, so this was the only way she could get things done downstairs when I wanted to lay in bed, which I've been doing a lot of lately.

"Alright, I'm heading downstairs. Is there anything you need?"

"Nope, I'm good! The games going to be on soon. Thanks, Gram!"

She stood in the doorway with her hands on her hips. "I don't really think you should call me that. That's disrespectful toward your grandmother."

"But I didn't even know my grandma, and you are like my grandmother. I'm sorry." I sank in my sheets, and Janice headed back over toward me.

"Oh, sweetie, it's okay. I just…well, never mind. If you want to call me that, call me "grandma." I won't get mad."

I smiled, looked up at her, and rested my head on her shoulder. My neck started was getting too heavy to hold up myself.

"I always wanted grandchildren. My only son never got married, though. But if I did, I would want them to be just like you and your sister."

"You are like our family now."

"Now, mister, don't make me cry." She rubbed my shoulder. I loved when she or Zoe did that. It felt good when my body hurt.

"Can you tell me the truth if I asked you a question?" I asked.

"Of course," she replied.

"Well, Zoe says I'm getting better, but I just have to take more medicine. I don't feel like I'm getting any better."

"Your sister's right. The doctors are giving you the medicine so you get better."

"But it makes me feel yucky, and my body really is starting to hurt more. Please don't tell Zoe that, though. I don't want her to worry anymore."

Janice looked like she was going to cry. "I won't. I promise. But you have to promise me that you'll get better."

"I'm trying. It's just hard. I can't even hold a book anymore." I went to reach for the book next to my bed but as I tried to grab it my grip released.

"I know, honey. But you just have to stay positive and keep praying that you will get better soon and you *will*. Now, is it almost game time?"

"It *is* game time!"

"I'll go downstairs now. Will you be okay?"

"I'll page you if I'm not, but I will be." I laid my head back down on the soft pillowcase as she turned the game on for me. I struggled with pressing the buttons.

Zoe is lucky she gets to work there. I've never been to a Siena basketball game before. Well, I've never been to a basketball game in person before. I really want to go, though, instead of watching it from my bed. It's just not the same. I imagine it being awesome. It's probably so loud there. I'd get a bag of popcorn and a soda and sit really close to the court. I would wear my Siena shirt and paint my face green like I see some kids do. Then I would cheer really loudly. Maybe one day I will get to do that. Maybe when I'm better.

"What's the score of the game?" Janice spoke through the walkie-talkie.

"Siena is down by three with thirteen minutes left in the first half, over."

"Roger that."

"Christian Michaels, three-pointer! And there we have it, ladies and gentlemen. The game is now tied. Quinnipiac runs the ball down the court, and the six-foot-four guard goes in for the lay up and—oh! Missed it! Saints get the ball back!"

"The tall guy with the blonde hair shoots and scores!"

"Janice?" I spoke quietly.

"Yeah?"

"No offense, but you didn't do that right."

{11}

Zoe

We won the game again. Christian was to thank for that. The game had ended ten minutes ago, which meant it was almost time for my second date. I didn't even know why I agreed to this. I went to the bathroom to fix my hair and make-up. I didn't have a change of clothes, so I had to take my time. Christian said to give him about a half hour after the game ended, and he would meet me out front.

It was another chilly night in the Capital Region. The low was supposed to be below zero, and with the wind chill, I didn't want to leave the building. I unfortunately forgot my gloves at home and didn't have time to go back and get them after I had realized.

My stomach churned. I was starving. I had no idea what Christian had in store for us tonight. Maybe he would take me to another place where an ex worked. I hated that I was so pessimistic about this, but I didn't see it ending well. Why did I even agree to go out again? I kept repeating that question over and over. Then I remembered it was because of Emily. I didn't even really want to go. I did, though. I just didn't want to admit it. I didn't want to admit it to myself or to them because that would mean I was starting to fall for him, which I couldn't be.

Sitting outside on the steps, I watched the cars drive by. As each minute passed, I began to grow more impatient. If he was going to be on time, he would be meeting me out here in only four more minutes. I made a deal with myself. If he was out here in four minutes, I would go. If he wasn't, I would leave. I would make up an excuse that I didn't feel well and drive home.

Three minutes were left. Cars continued to drive by, and, I swear, in that one minute the temperature dropped significantly. It all seemed pretty surreal to me. Thinking back on the past few weeks, I didn't imagine myself even dating, at least not until Gabe was better. Maybe not even until I was finished with school.

Snow fell from the sky. The touch of the light snowflakes on my bare hands made them colder. I buried them in my jacket pockets to try and keep them warm. Continuing to watch the street in front of me, people were leaving the bar that was just outside of the arena. A couple in particular stood out to me. You could tell by watching them that they were genuinely happy. She walked outside laughing, her head lying on his shoulder as he held her hand. They walked to the car parked across the street. Opening the door for her, he kissed her on the forehead and shut the door behind her as she sat in.

I wasn't sure if I was more jealous or scared. As much as I wanted something like that, I was also terrified. I didn't know what it felt like to love and to be loved. Seeing my friends be happy and then completely heartbroken and going through that over and over again scared me. I don't want that to happen to me. But I remember my parents' relationship, and they were always happy. I don't know of a time that they ever argued.

After getting lost in my thoughts, I looked down at my phone. There was only a minute left until Christian said he would meet me.

{12}

Christian

I didn't think the game would ever end. I loved playing basketball, so I never thought I would see the day that I would want to do something more. But today was just that. The entire game the only thing I could think about was my second date with Zoe.

After the game, I quickly showered and began to get ready. I told her I would meet her a half an hour after the game ended. That was my estimate, anyway. After the game ended, our coach would talk to us for, on average, ten to fifteen minutes, then I would meet with a reporter for five minutes, then showering and getting ready shouldn't take me much longer than that. I should be out there just in time.

Tonight was going to be perfect. I wanted to make up for the first date. Since it was so cold out, I planned to take Zoe to a small bakery closer to school. It closed hours before the game, but I knew the owners well, and after telling them what I wanted to do, they agreed without hesitation. I'm going to bring her there, and a table will be set for two with a candle lit in the middle. A fire will be burning in the fireplace, and the bakery would be lit up with Christmas lights. Thanks to Zoe's friend, I found out what her favorite dessert was and had the owners prepare it for her. Luckily, I was able to do this on a whim and under short notice. I wanted it to be romantic. I had planned this earlier in the day, taking a good chance that she would accept my date invitation.

However, everything seemed to be going wrong. Anxiety was thriving inside of me now. Our coach talked for longer than usual, and tonight, not one, but two reporters wanted to talk to me. Their interviews were longer than usual too. I should have known that everyone would want to talk after this big win. We defeated the number one team in the conference. Everyone called tonight's game the MAAC Championship Finals preview. My phone was trapped in the locker room, and I didn't have access to it until after I was done with the interviews. I had no idea what time it was.

Entering the locker room in a rush, I scrambled through my stuff to reach my phone. Good. I had 10 minutes to shower and get ready. I decided to text Zoe to let her know I might be a few minutes longer so I didn't make her worry.

I ran my hand through my semi-wet hair, buttoned my shirt, and threw on my jacket. Zipping up my bag and collecting all of my things, I ran out of the locker room. The path from the locker room to where I said I would meet her seemed longer than I remembered. The arena was empty by now, which made it easier for me to run a straight path. I raced down the court, and found my way to where I would meet her.

I got to the door and saw through the glass a girl sitting on the very steps where she said she was. Her hood was up, and her hands were tucked in her jacket. It was dark out, but no one else was here. My heart was racing, and I saw my reflection in the door. I was smiling. This girl was doing more to me than I had realized, and I still barely knew her.

Opening the door, I walked quickly toward her.

"Zoe! Sorry. I tried to get ready as fast as I could!"

The girl turned around and stared at me.

It wasn't Zoe.

I looked down at my phone to see if she had texted me, and I had a new text from her from about five minutes ago. Looking at our conversation, I felt awful. My text to her about being later than I thought I would was still typed out as a draft. I never hit send.

"I'm an idiot," I said aloud and threw my bag onto the ground. The girl who I mistakenly called Zoe continued to stare.

"I'm sorry. I thought you were someone else." I quickly picked up my bag and walked toward my car.

She texted me to tell me she didn't feel well and wanted to go home and sleep. As much as I wanted to believe it, I had left her sitting there thinking I probably wasn't coming because again I was late without letting her know. She probably thought I was ditching her. I picked up my phone and called her.

No answer.

I wondered how long she was even waiting for or if she decided not to come all-together.

"I really thought tonight was going to be perfect," I mumbled under my breath while I threw my bag in the back of my car before speeding off.

{13}

Gabe

"How was your night last night?" I asked Zoe. She entered my room with breakfast so I could eat it in bed. This was my favorite part of the weekend. She made the best pancakes!

"I didn't go. I didn't feel well."

"Oh, that sucks. I'm sorry. Are you feeling better today? What's wrong? Where were you supposed to go anyways?" I fell asleep early last night, even before the game ended, which was probably why I didn't hear her come home early.

"Just out with some friends."

"Friends? What friends were you going out with?" She always told me who she was going out with.

"Some from school," she replied. Okay, now she's not telling me something.

"You never go out with friends from school."

"Well, I was going to."

"But you didn't. Why?" She was hiding something from me.

"I said I didn't feel well."

"Oh. So are you feeling better now? You seem fine to me."

"Yes, much better. I think it was something I ate. In fact, since I wasn't home to hang out with you last night before you went to sleep, how about I take you out today for a special treat?"

She wanted to take me out for a special treat, and she made me pancakes. She was definitely hiding something. Zoe has been too afraid to take me places since I've become more sick. What was she lying to me about?

"Where are we going?" I asked.

"We're going to go to the store. I'm going to buy you ice cream of your choice and as many toppings as you want to make an ice cream sundae. You can pick out movies too. We will have a ice cream and a movies day!"

"Yay! I love when you let me eat ice cream!" I was going to get to the bottom of this. Zoe never lied to me, but I had to go along with it. If I kept questioning her now she might back out on getting me ice cream, and I really wanted ice cream.

"I love ice cream too! So how about you eat these pancakes, and I will help you get ready and we can go to the store."

Since my body has gotten weaker, I have had to use a wheelchair when we go places. I used to hate going to the store, but now I loved it because I sometimes saw people I knew and I was actually out of the house. I also got to ride around in my cool wheelchair and show it off. People by now knew I was sick, so I wasn't embarrassed anymore.

"I want cookies and cream and peanut butter."

"Just one flavor," Zoe demanded.

"Please, please, pretty please?" I begged. I wanted a few scoops of each. I put on my puppy dog face and looked her in the eye—the face she could never say no to. I had some tricks she hasn't caught onto yet.

"Just one. How about cookies and cream, and you can get peanut butter cups to go on top?"

"Ok, I guess." I stopped arguing. That did sound really good.

The next aisle had all the candy. I didn't know how to pick what I wanted! I could go with what she said, but there was just so much!

"Don't go anywhere. I have to go grab a basket really quick so we can carry everything."

"Ok, I need to decide anyways."

"Good! Don't move!" she insisted. I don't know where she thinks I would go, though.

I stared at the candy. There were mini peanut butter cups, gummy bears, chocolate chips, marshmallows—it was never ending. How was I ever going to choose? I wanted it all. But I knew Zoe wouldn't let me get it all. I needed to have a healthy diet since I was so sick. I couldn't push the treat she was allowing me to have. I decided I wanted the marshmallows. I tried to reach them, but I couldn't from my wheelchair.

"Do you need help? Is this what you wanted? Here you go," a man said handing me the candy.

"Thank you!" I placed the candy in my lap and looked up to see the man who helped me. "Oh! You're...you're..." I was so excited I couldn't talk. I couldn't get the words out of my mouth, I was so surprised.

"I'm Christian Michaels! Nice to meet you." He said shaking my hand. "I see you like Siena basketball?"

"Yes! I am your biggest fan! See? I am even wearing your shirt!" I unzipped my jacket to show him. He was even taller in person, but he bent down to his knees to level with me.

"What are you buying?" He asked.

"Toppings. My sister is treating me to ice cream sundaes today, and I get to pick anything I want to put on it. She just went to get a basket. You have to meet her! She actually goes to Siena. She won't believe me unless you stay. Please? She will be right back!"

I wanted Zoe to meet him. Maybe I could invite him over to have ice cream with us. I couldn't believe I just met Christian Michaels.

"Gabe, are you okay?" Zoe shouted from down the aisle. His back was to her, so she was probably making sure no stranger was being mean to me. She got nervous like that sometimes.

"Look who it is!" I yelled. Christian stood up and turned around.

"Zoe?" Christian stuttered.

I curled my lips in and my eyebrows sank into my skin. I thought to myself, "how did Christian know my sister's name?" She didn't tell me she knew him!

"How are you feeling? Sorry about last night," Christian said.

"How did he know you were sick?" I asked out loud. "You're friends with him and never told me? How could you? Wait. Is this your secret?" I whispered.

"I was supposed to take your sister out last night," Christian replied to Gabe.

"I'm sorry, but we have to get going," Zoe said in a weird tone. I don't know why she wanted to leave so quickly. Didn't she know who we were talking to?

"But wait! If you were supposed to hang out last night, maybe he can come over today since you are feeling better!"

"That's not a good idea," Zoe replied quickly and put her hands on the back of my wheelchair to push me away.

"Why not?" I asked, looking up at her.

"Yeah, why not?" Christian agreed. He was smirking and gave me a wink.

"I...I..." Zoe hesitated.

"I can come over and bring more toppings for those sundaes! I was actually about to buy some peanut butter ice cream too, so you will have two flavors to choose from." Christian added.

"Oh my God! I wanted that flavor too! Zoe, can he please come? Pretty, pretty please?" I whined. When I started to whine, Zoe always gave in, especially if we were in public. She didn't want to make a scene.

"I don't know. He's probably busy."

"I'm not. I have no plans today, actually," he replied.

"See?" I said, trying to get a response out of Zoe.

Zoe stared at Christian for a while before finally agreeing and giving him our address. Wow! Today is going to be so much fun. I can't believe Christian Michaels will be coming over to my house! For a moment I forgot my body had even been aching today. I forgot how sick I was. This was like a dream come true. The person I've dreamed about being when I'm older was going to be hanging out with me.

How could Zoe not tell me she was friends with him?

{14}

Zoe

Gabe didn't stop talking the entire car ride home from the store. I would be naive to say that I wasn't expecting him to act this way. Was it selfish of me for trying to avoid this? As much as I loved seeing Gabe this animated, I was trying to prevent the inevitable from happening. If Christian left our lives, it would destroy Gabe. He didn't seem like the type of guy to want to be involved in the kind of life I lived.

Watching out the window, I stared blankly out at the driveway. He texted me a few minutes ago to let me know that he was on his way. I had no idea what to expect out of tonight. I panicked.

"Gabe, I'm going upstairs for a minute. If he gets here, let him in?"

"Of course!" Gabe shouted excitedly. He hadn't left the living room since we got home.

I ran upstairs to my bathroom. Gripping both sides of the sink, I looked down and closed my eyes. Taking a few deep breaths, I looked up into the mirror.

"Tonight is going to go fine. It's going to be okay. It's just a movie and ice cream. Gabe is here. We aren't alone. It's going to go great. Everything is going to be fine." I was talking to myself hoping that I could talk myself out of the nervousness. Panic attacks had become more frequent because of my lack of sleep and the stress I have been under.

Daddy, I wish you were here. Is Christian a good guy? Would you approve? Is he the guy you once told me would come into my life and sweep me off my feet? I need answers.

I couldn't stop thinking about how my dad would act if he were still here. Thoughts like if he would approve of a guy coming over, if he would ask him a million questions, or what age he would have allowed me to first date.

Then I thought, *How would my mom be acting? Would I tell her everything? Would I tell her how I felt about him?* I envied some of my friends for the relationships they had with their parents and for the things their parents were around to see and watch as they grew up.

The doorbell rang.

I stood at the top of the stairs, listening to the conversation below me.

"So what movie are we watching tonight?" Christian asked Gabe as he walked through the door.

"I'm not sure yet. I figured since you were our guest you could pick!" He lowered his voice and continued, "Zoe told me to say that."

"How about we let your sister pick?"

"I'm not too sure about that one. She can never make up her mind, and well, if we let her pick, we will probably be stuck here watching some girly movie."

"Oh, you know, that's a very good point you make."

"Yeah, don't want to get stuck watching those with her!"

"Well, you're in luck. I did bring a few movies I thought you might want to watch. Where is your sister, anyway?"

"Zoe! Christian is here!" Gabe shouted from downstairs. "Now she'll come quickly," he said to Christian, not realizing I could hear their entire conversation.

I waited a few moments before heading down the stairs so I wouldn't seem too anxious. Looking down, I saw Christian sitting there close to Gabe showing him a selection of movies. He seemed to get more attractive every time I saw him. That, or I was starting to fall for him. The two of them were smiling, and this was the happiest I have seen Gabe in a very long time.

Maybe Christian was a good guy after all?

I was so wrapped up in looking at the two of them interacting, I completely missed a step near the bottom the stairs. Falling on my butt, I slid down the rest of the way making a loud noise as I hit each step. Silence filled the living room until the two of them burst out laughing.

I stood up, horrified.

"Are you okay?" Christian asked, barely able to get the words out from laughing so hard with Gabe.

"Yes. We really need to get a rug on those stairs. They're really slick, especially with socks on." Christian looked down, noticing my fuzzy socks I had put on.

"There's so much we need to do in this house. I have to add that to the top of the list," I added.

"This is a beautiful house! What do your parents do for a living?" Christian asked.

Before I could say anything Gabe spoke up quickly. "My daddy's in heaven, and we don't know where my mom is." A pit arose in my stomach.

Christian looked over at me with a glimmer of sadness on his face and turned back to Gabe.

"Well, you have an amazing sister who I'm sure takes great care of you!"

"She does everything for me," Gabe responded, and I knew Christian was starting to see a little bit of what my life was like.

"So I brought a few movies. Gabe said you would pick out a bad movie, so looks like you will just have to settle for something we choose. Right, Gabe?" Christian said with a smirk, changing the subject.

Gabe laughed. "Yeah, Zoe, we don't want to watch a girly movie."

"Okay, okay, guys. I guess I will have to settle for your choice."

"I was thinking Home Alone? It's one of my favorites," Christian suggested.

"That is a great movie," I agreed while looking over to Gabe to see what he thought.

"I haven't ever seen it before!" He picked it up and looked at the case.

"What! Is your sister depriving you?"

"Yeah, Zoe, stop depriving me. What does depriving mean?"

"Okay, you two, I see you have teamed up against me already! What's up with that?"

"Nothing." Gabe laughed and pounded fists with Christian.

By now I was probably grinning from ear to ear, but I couldn't help it. I wanted nothing more than for Gabe to be happy. Watching him and Christian interact was truly amazing. He was so good to him. Maybe I was wrong about Christian after all.

{15}

Christian

"How am I still hungry?" Zoe laughed, and her smile lit up the entire room.

"I was just thinking the same thing! How about I grab more ice cream? How much do you want?"

"Bring two spoons and the carton. I promise I'm not a pig!" We both continued to laugh.

I brought the ice cream back into the room, listening to her suggestion. This enabled me to sit closer to her since we were sharing. The night just continued to get better.

"I wouldn't be surprised if we finish this off tonight. Gabe won't be happy, but this is so good," Zoe said while taking in another spoonful of ice cream.

"Gabe seems like a really great kid!" After being around her and Gabe tonight, I really missed all of the good times I had with my brother.

"He is, especially after everything he has gone through. The kid is so strong."

"Can I ask what happened? Why he's in the wheelchair, I mean? It's okay if you don't want to talk about it."

Zoe looked at me, and just seeing the way her emotions changed I could tell things weren't good. A knot formed in my stomach, and I realized I cared for her already more than I probably should. Gabe mentioned earlier that his father had died and their mom wasn't around. That sentence ran through my head, and I couldn't help but admire how strong Zoe appeared to be for everything she has been through. Worried to hear what she was about to say, I shoved another spoonful of ice cream in my mouth.

"I knew this would be brought up eventually. You see, my family has gone through a lot in the last seven or so years. Gabe is sick. He's really sick." She looked down at her feet.

"What do you mean, sick? Cancer?" I questioned.

"Yeah. Leukemia."

Instinctively I took her hand, which, surprisingly, didn't catch her off guard.

"Zoe, I'm so, so sorry." I felt for her. I knew what it was like to lose a brother, but I can't even imagine losing my parents too.

"We found out about three years ago when he was in kindergarten. Things were already a mess, and it just continued to get worse. Right after Gabe was born, my father passed away. My mom didn't handle it well. She got sick, but in a different kind of way. She had a broken heart, and nothing could cure it. She had become mentally ill. When Gabe was diagnosed and the money situation became more difficult for us, she left. Now it's even harder, but we get by. Gabe's attitude is amazing for a kid that has gone through so much. I like to believe that his good spirits are what keep him going. He is still going through treatments, so he's out of school for now. Dr. Sheehan is hopeful he'll fight this. The money has been hard for us; hence I am always working. I just want to be able to spend more time with him. I feel so bad."

Zoe stopped talking. I was at a loss for words. I flashbacked to how I felt after James died.

"I'm sorry. I know that was a lot; I didn't mean to let it all out like that. I just don't talk about it a lot," Zoe said, letting her hand go from mine and placing it in her lap.

I grabbed her hand back quickly, and brought her in closer to me.

"I lost my brother in an accident." My voice cracked while I spoke.

"I didn't know that. I'm sorry." Her eyes widened.

"Not many people do. I don't really talk about it either."

"How old was he?"

"A freshman in college. He had just started at Siena. It was the reason I chose to go here. Loss is a horrible thing. I'm sorry you have had to go through it too—more than I have, I mean." Our shared grief seemed to bring us closer together.

"I'm sorry too. Not many of my friends have experienced a close loss like I have. It's kind of nice to know I'm not the only one for once."

"You're right. You're not alone. I know we hardly know each other, but I'm always here to talk if you need me." I rubbed my thumb in a circular motion on her hand and she let her head drop down on my shoulder.

"I just hope I don't lose Gabe. He's all I have left. I can't lose him. I just can't." Her eyes were teary.

"You won't lose him. What else can they do?" I said, pulling her in even closer to me.

"Not much. Not much at all. It would be easier if they could find a bone marrow donor, but I'm not a match, and they haven't been able to find one in the donor system yet. I'm scared that by the time they find one, it'll be too late."

A powerful gust of wind blew inside through the window, putting out the only source of light. The flames of the fire quickly died, and darkness filled the room. Through the silence I could now hear her breathe, and I watched her shoulders rise as she inhaled deeply. Placing my thumb on her cheek, I wiped away the visible tears that began to fall. A few tears had soon become a film of water covering her glowing green eyes. Slowly moving my hand to the edge of her face, I brushed away the hairs that fell in front of her lips. Our eyes met, and a sudden burst of heat rushed through all of the limbs in my body. As I closed my eyes, our lips touched for the first time. I kissed her, and my heart started to beat like a runaway train, faster and faster.

{16}

Zoe

I walked Christian to the front door. I didn't want him to leave.

"I had a great time tonight," we both said in sync. Laughing, he bent his head down to kiss me once more. Our lips were barely touching when a sound came from the living room.

"Wait here," Christian whispered while placing his finger on my lip.

I took a step back and smiled again. Walking into the living room, I watched him slide his arms underneath Gabe, who was sound asleep. Picking him up, he headed over toward the stairs.

"He should be in his bed. Which room is his?"

I smiled and walked him toward Gabe's room.

Lying him down in his bed, Christian covered Gabe up under his blankets and gently placed his head on his pillow.

"Stay strong, buddy. If not for me, do it for your sister," Christian whispered before exiting his room.

He kissed me again as we got down the stairs, and I could feel my heart beating out of my chest.

"You didn't have to do that. For Gabe, I mean."

"I wanted to. Have a good night, Zoe. I hope to see you

again soon." He held my hand and kissed me on my cheek before shutting the door behind him. I stood there for a moment before heading up to bed.

How was I so wrong about him?

*

Once again I laid awake at three in the morning, restless and covered in sweat. I couldn't sleep. Waking up in a panic with tears streaming down my face had become a common occurrence lately. The dreams were all different except for one detail that never changed, that one tiny detail that sent my heart racing. Gabe was in the hospital. Dying.

The negative changes in his health overpowered the positive, which, in turn, made my fear of losing Gabe more evident. The recurring dreams stemmed from the negative thoughts I couldn't shut out. Christian made his first appearance tonight in these nightmares. Standing by my side next to Gabe's hospital bed, he took my hand like he did before I fell asleep, sending energy quickly through my bloodstream like a fire upon a gas encoded stick.

As I lay awake in bed, I continued to replay the dream and the events that occurred hours before I went to sleep. I soon found myself wondering how my life went from so perfect to a constant battle between finding my own happiness and making everyone else happy. I grabbed the picture that stood still on my nightstand and held it close to my pounding heart.

The little girl in the picture had a smile so wide her eyes were shut. It was easy to recognize that she was laughing and really happy. Her dad was right behind her, pretending to push the swing but clearly posing for the picture. The happiness that thrived between the two of them wasn't fake. I looked down at the picture and stared at it. I tried to remember what being happy like that felt like, what it felt like to not have to worry about anything.

I can remember that day like it was yesterday. My dad and I were out in the back on the swings, as seen in the picture. My mom came out of the back door calling for us to come inside.

"Let's just tell her now!" my father exclaimed.

"Are you sure?" my mother asked, smiling, and took out her camera.

"Zoe, your mother and I have some good news we'd like to share with you."

The best part about that day had become the very moment the words escaped from his lips. I was going to be a big sister. It was the best day of my life.

Setting the picture back over onto my nightstand, time seemed to get away from me. It was already 5:30 in the morning. My shift at my other job started at seven, which meant I only had a few more minutes to lay in bed. Getting off of my pillow top mattress was a struggle. There was nothing more comfortable than a warm bed in the winter. Finally pushing my body above the bed and placing my feet onto the rug, I headed downstairs.

I stopped next to the kitchen to rub my eyes as I yawned, but a sudden noise sent my feet off the ground.

Peeking around the corner, a sigh of relief let loose from my mouth when I discovered it was only Janice.

"Looks like you had a busy night last night. I hope you didn't eat all of this by yourself!" She studied the empty cartons next to the sink along with the dirty bowls.

"Christian came over," I said under my breath.

"Oh sweetie, that's great! Things must be going really well. I thought you weren't going to tell Gabe?"

"I wasn't. We ran into him in the store, and well, the two of them teamed up against me. Things went surprisingly well!"

I sat down at the kitchen table, and continued to tell her about the events that occurred last night over a cup of coffee. Starting with Christian's arrival, I told her how Gabe wouldn't stop talking the entire time, and about the clear bond between the two of them.

"Gabe sat there and talked to him the entire night. Every question he wanted to ask Christian about basketball, he did. So Christian offered to teach him a few things when he was better. He was so sweet with him. "

"Does he know about Gabe's illness?" Janice asked.

"When Gabe went to sleep I told him everything." I muttered. I still had a hard time believing it myself.

"Everything?" she questioned, wanting to know more.

"Yes. Everything. Even about Mom and Dad. I don't know what got into me. I just had a sudden feeling that I could trust him, and before I knew it, it all came out of my mouth. He lost his brother at a young age too. We really seemed to connect last night, even if it had to do with unfortunate circumstances."

"That's not a bad thing, Zoe. I told you the right guy was going to come around soon, that you would just know. You just have to allow yourself to be open to opportunities like this and stop being so nervous."

"Wait, I haven't even gotten to the best part. Before Christian left, do you want to know what he did? I keep visualizing it in my head. I can't stop thinking about it."

"He kissed you?" Janice laughed.

"Yes," I hesitated, "but that's not it."

"Well?" Janice asked.

"He really cares about Gabe. I could see it in his eyes, the way he spoke to him. He even carried him upstairs to bed."

"Look at that smile on your face!" Janice and I laughed in happiness.

How could I have fallen so quickly in just one night?

{17}

Christian

"Hi, I need to speak to Dr. Sheehan."

"What's your name?" the receptionist asked.

"Christian Michaels."

"Do you have an appointment?"

"Not exactly."

"You need to make an appointment first." She looked back toward her computer.

"I just need to talk to her for ten minutes. It's important."

"I'm sure it is, but Dr. Sheehan has a busy schedule today."

"Can you ask her if I can see her? Tell her it's regarding Gabe Gingras."

"Have a seat." She didn't sound too thrilled.

I was about to turn around to find a seat when I felt someone tugging on the back of my sweatshirt.

"Excuse me." I turned around at the sound of the quiet voice.

"Excuse me. Are you Christian Michaels?" The little boy continued.

"Yes, I am. What can I do for you?" I bent down to his level.

"Mom! It is him!" He yelled across the waiting room to a woman with dark curly long hair who motioned for him to come back to her.

"Can I get a picture?"

"Sure thing!"

"Mom! He said he'll take a picture with me!" He grabbed my hand and ran toward her.

I bent down next to him and wrapped my arm around his shoulders.

"Say cheese," the mother said, and we both smiled.

"What do you say?" She looked at her son as her eyebrows lifted.

"Thank you!" The little boy gave me a big hug and ran off to grab a book from the shelf.

"Thank you for making his day a little brighter."

"Not a problem," I responded before sitting down. I watched the little boy pick out a few books and play with the toys. His hat fell off, and I saw his bald head. *How could so many little kids be affected by something so terrible?*

"Mr. Michaels?" the receptionist yelled out. "Mr. Michaels?"

My mind had been wandering off, thinking about what these kids have to go through each day and all of the challenges they must face.

"Mr. Michaels!" I stood up quickly.

"Sorry, I'm here."

"Dr. Sheehan said she can see you quickly. Follow me."

I was nervous. I didn't even know what I was doing here. When I woke up this morning, the only thing that was on my mind other than Zoe was helping Gabe.

"Wait in here. She'll be right in." She closed the door behind her.

I looked around. All of Dr. Sheehan's degrees and certificates were framed on the wall. On her desk were pictures of her family. The wall to my right had brochures for different treatments and informative packets about acute leukemia. As I bent down to itch my leg, my eyes caught sight of the vents along the bottom of the wall. I had another idea.

"So what can I do for you, Mr. Michaels?" Dr. Sheehan opened the door and sat down at the desk in front of me.

"I just had a few questions about Gabe Gingras."

"Unfortunately, I can't give you any information since you aren't immediate family. What is your relation to him?"

"I'm a friend of Zoe's. Can you actually keep this meeting between us? She doesn't know I'm here."

"Why are you here?" She leaned in closer and her right eyebrow lifted.

"I want to help Gabe. Is there anything I can do? Zoe mentioned the treatments are expensive."

Dr. Sheehan smiled at the conclusion of my proposal.

"Yes, there is. I can give you this packet, which will give you a general idea of what the treatments cost for cancer patients with and without insurance."

"Ok, great. Thank you." I flipped through the pages.

"So you really want to help?" She took off her glasses and looked into my eyes with sincerity.

"I do. I really do."

"Zoe never mentioned you before, and neither did Gabe. Everyone here knows how big of a Siena fan Gabe is."

I smiled.

"I only started hanging out with Zoe not too long ago, but I've grown to really care about the both of them. Gabe's awesome."

"He's one of my best patients. He really admires you. He tells me every visit how badly he wants to go to a Siena basketball game. He won't give up. Unfortunately, he's been so weak it would be too exhausting for him."

"I know you can't give me much information, but is there anything medically I can do? What about my chances of being his bone marrow donor? Zoe mentioned that would be his best shot of beating this but that there hasn't been a match."

"That's always a possibility. We can certainly do the testing to see if you would be a match and a proper donor, but if you do it's going to limit your physical activity. If you appear to be a match through DNA we will have to prep you, which can be physically draining for some people."

"What does that entail?" I questioned.

"You will have to have additional blood tests and physical exams spread out over a four to six week period to make sure that you are the best donor for Gabe."

"Okay, that's not a problem. How do I get tested?"

"I can do a cheek swab to test your DNA against his to see if it matches the six basic HLA markers."

"Let's do that. How long will it take to get the results back?"

"Not too long. But Christian, are you sure about this?"

"One hundred percent. And please don't tell Zoe about this," I said confidently.

{18}

Gabe

"Ugh!" I crinkled up my paper and brushed the markers off of the table so they hit the floor.

The red marker rolled until it hit the back of Janice's foot.

"What's wrong Gabe?"

"I can't do it!" I yelled.

"What can't you do?" she said sweetly while placing her hand on my shoulder.

Pushing her hand away, I laid my head down on the table.

"I just wanted to make Zoe a nice drawing to surprise her. But..." I couldn't hold it in. I started to cry.

"But what?" Janice picked up the markers and placed them on the table.

"My hands hurt, and they're shaky, and it's not coming out right. It doesn't look good. Zoe won't even like it."

"Oh sweetie, she would like anything you make her."

"But I want to make something nice for once!" I sniffled and wiped my tears and my nose with my sleeve.

"Here. Let me get you a tissue, and then I can help you."

Just as Janice handed me the box of tissues, the doorbell rang.

"Why is someone here?" I questioned as she walked to the door.

"Gabe, looks like you have a visitor!"

I wiped the tears from my eyes and lifted my head up a bit from the table when I heard her talking with a familiar voice.

"Christian!" I sat up fast. Too fast. My head spun a bit.

"Hey, buddy!"

"What are you doing here? Zoe's working."

"Oh, she is? That's okay. We can hang out today. Just the two of us. How does that sound?"

"Really?"

"Yes, really! What are you working on?"

"I was drawing a picture for Zoe, but I messed up."

"Maybe I can help? I used to be really good in art class."

I looked over at Janice, who was smiling in the corner of the kitchen.

"I would like that."

"Okay, how about you start it, and I'll help you when I'm done."

"Done with what?"

"I came over to fix the vents so that way it's not so cold in here." I saw he was holding a tool kit.

"Oh, Zoe will be happy."

"Gabe, would it be okay if I left you with Christian for a while? I need to run out to the store," Janice asked.

"That's fine! We'll be okay."

"Yes, we will." Christian fist bumped me.

Janice left, and he went to go fix our heat problem. I started to draw again, but my hands were starting to shake. I was drawing a sunrise over an ocean, Zoe's favorite thing.

Picking up the blue marker to start coloring the water, I couldn't get the cap off. It was really hard for me to pull it off. I wasn't strong enough anymore. I even tried with my teeth.

I sat back in my chair and stared at the paper and the marker. I didn't want Christian to see how weak I was.

"Christian, how do you get stronger?"

He walked toward me and set his wrench down on the table.

"Well, strength training and eating lots of protein. You eat your meat, don't you?"

"Yes, but…but I'm getting weaker from being so sick, and I want to get stronger." I looked down toward the floor.

"You will! I believe in you." Christian put his hand on my shoulder.

"Do you believe that God answers prayers?" I asked him.

"I do. Do you?"

"I think he answered one of mine." I smiled and tilted my head on my arm. I was starting to get tired.

"What was that?"

"I asked him to make Zoe happy. She's so upset since I'm so sick. But I overheard her talking to Janice, and she said you make her really happy."

"She said that?" Christian smiled.

"Yeah, she did. I think God brought you into our lives to make her happy."

"I think so too. Now, what are we going to draw for her?"

"I wanted to draw the sunrise over the ocean."

"Well, first you have to draw the horizon."

Christian took a pencil and drew a line across the center of the paper.

*

I finished the drawing with Christian's help. Zoe's going to love it! He really knew what he was talking about. Having him around felt like I had a brother too.

"Yes! I win!" I shouted.

"You are just too good! I will win next time. Rematch?" Christian suggested. We were playing NCAA on my PS3.

Just as I was about to press play, I could hear the front door open downstairs.

"Hello?" Zoe called out.

"Shh, Zoe's home." Christian put his finger over his mouth.

"Where are you?"

I hid underneath my covers. Christian hid on the other side of my bed.

"Hmm, where could Gabe be? Is he in the closet?" She opened the closet doors.

"Nope, not in there. What about underneath the bed?"

Zoe got down on the ground but jumped up in panic.

"Oh my God! Shit, Christian you scared me!"

I laughed underneath my covers.

"Did we get you good?" I giggled.

"Yes, you did!"

Christian and I laughed, and he gave me a high five.

"What are you doing here? I didn't see your car."

"I parked around the corner so you wouldn't see it."

"He fixed our vents and was hanging out with me all day."

I looked over at Zoe and back to Christian. They were both staring at each other and wouldn't stop. Finally Zoe smiled.

"Did you really?" Zoe said quietly.

"Hey, Gabe, do you mind if I go and talk to your sister for a minute? Then I'll come back in and we can finish our game."

"Sure!"

I sat in my bed and tried to listen to their conversation in the hallway, but it was too low to hear. Today was such a good day. I really like having him around.

"Thank you, God, for making my sister happy. Now please keep her happy. I don't like seeing her upset. It's not fair to her when she does so much for me. Thank you for bringing Chris into our lives, and please let me win when I play him in this game, I really, really want to win." I prayed quietly.

{19}

Zoe

Emily wanted to know all of the details. I haven't had a chance to hang out with her outside of classes because my schedule has been so busy, and I refused to tell her anything over the phone.

I started to tell her everything that has happened as we put out the bobble-heads on the tables for today's game. It was a giveaway night.

"I don't even know where to start. So much has happened."

"We have two hours before the game and a whole lot of bobble-heads to put out. I think you can get through all of it. Just start from what happened after the last game we worked together and don't leave anything out. Remember who is watching Gabe for you tonight so you can go out." Emily was so excited she could barely hold it in.

I filled her in, starting with how I skipped the date he had planned and the events that followed the next day—running into him at the store, telling him about Gabe, our first kiss. And then I got into every time we've hung out since then, which has been a lot.

"The day he came over and surprised me and fixed the vents, I watched how he interacted with Gabe, and I couldn't stop smiling.

It was the moment fell for him, or at least the moment I realized I was I was falling for him." I smiled.

"I don't want to say I told you so, but…" Emily and I laughed.

"Yes, you were right to give him a chance! That Wednesday night after practice he showed up and surprised me with dinner. Tuesday and Thursday I stayed home with Gabe, and we streamed the games on the TV through my computer. Christian made it a point to text me right before each game and as soon as he could after. There hasn't been a day he hasn't texted me. Not even a day went by this week without receiving a good morning text from him."

"You know how much I love good morning texts." She stopped putting the bobble-heads on the table and listened intently.

"Well, the last two weeks we have just been hanging out a lot and doing a lot of…kissing." I couldn't stop smiling as I continued to tell her everything. Just thinking about him brought a smile to my face.

"Zoe, this is getting serious." Emily stared at me with a huge grin, and I didn't disagree. It was moving quick, but I didn't even care. I leaned against the table and sighed.

"I haven't even finished with the rest of this past weekend yet."

"So keep going."

"Friday after I got out of work, he was already at my house. He had a present for Gabe. It was a basketball signed by the entire team. Emily, I have never seen Gabe so happy before. When you see him tonight, I'm sure he will tell you all about it. That night all Christian wanted to do was play games with Gabe. I was so wrong about him. He has been amazing and such a good guy. Sometimes I wonder if he is even at my house to see me or Gabe."

"This is amazing, Zoe! He sounds perfect for you, and you sound like you really, really like him. So where are you going tonight?"

"I do," I smiled, "and I have no idea." I thought about it for a minute. Not knowing where I was headed gave me a bit of anxiety.

"You don't know?"

"No. He said it was a surprise. Again. He's very enigmatic."

"Hm. I wonder what he has planned."

"Me too! Thanks for watching Gabe tonight. I didn't want to bother Janice because I didn't know how late we will be, and she's been over a lot more lately."

"It's no problem at all! Gabe and I will have fun!"

*

The game seemed to fly right by. As I walked to my car, I couldn't stop thinking about Christian. The entire game I had sat there with my eyes glued on him. Every now and then he would catch me looking at him, so he'd flash me his gorgeous smile.

How did I get so lucky? How did I get to this point? Is this too good to be true?

I thought of all the girls who had been in the arena today who had their eyes on Christian too, admiring how attractive he was and his talent. Lacey, his ex-girlfriend, couldn't take her eyes off of him either. She was beautiful. I glanced over at her a few times. Something about her made me uneasy, but he's taking me out tonight. He broke up with her and is now with me. I never in a million years would have thought something like this would be happening in my life.

At the end of the game, he had motioned for me to check my phone before walking off of the court from their win. A few moments later he texted me.

"Meet me at this address in about an hour." I looked back at this text again.

Looking at the address, it didn't look familiar. I've lived here my entire life and I've never heard of this street. After putting it into my GPS, it looked like it was in the middle of nowhere.

Where is he taking me?

*

Arriving at the location, my observations were right. I was literally in the middle of nowhere. Christian looked like he had just pulled in a few minutes before I did. Turning his car off and opening his door, he stepped out onto the snow-covered gravel. Behind his vehicle was a trailer. I wondered what that's for.

"You didn't take me here to kill me, did you? Where are we?" I joked with him.

"Have you ever been snowmobile riding before?"

"No, I haven't." Looking down at my outfit, I wasn't exactly dressed to go riding either.

"Don't worry. We won't be for long. We just need one to get to our destination. Here." He took his jacket off of his back and handed it to me. "Wear this so you don't get too cold."

Opening up the back of the trailer, he hopped on the snowmobile that was inside and backed it off onto the ground.

"Is this yours?"

"No. No, we don't even have these in the city; there's nowhere to ride. I borrowed it. Alpin Haus is a sponsor of the basketball team, so I was able to use one for the night. I met the owner a while back, so he cut me a good deal. Here, put this on." He handed me a helmet this time. I did not think we would be outside tonight.

Throwing the helmet on, I have to admit I was nervous. I had never ridden on one before, and I didn't even know anything was out here. I was curious where we were going. Sitting behind Christian, I threw my hands around his waist, holding on tight as he held down the gas lever. Nausea overcame me. I'm not sure if it was more because of my fear of not knowing where we were or that I was hungry. I just assumed we were grabbing food, so I hadn't eaten in a few hours.

We drove for about fifteen minutes. My eyes were drawn to anything that looked like a destination, but there were only a few houses that I could make out in the distance. We drove through trails in the woods, across an iced over pond, and up several hills. Going over another and much larger pond, he slowed down. I soon was able to identify a large cabin up ahead. As we got closer, I noticed that it was lit up with Christmas lights. A few more snowmobiles were parked in the front of the cabin.

"What is this place?"

"You'll see." Christian remained mysterious. "Are you ready to go in?"

"As ready as I'll ever be, I guess," I responded under my breath with nervousness.

We stepped up to the door. Before Christian could grab the handle, a man opened it.

"Mr. Michaels, you made it! Your table is ready over there. Follow me."

Where are we?

{20}

Christian

I watched the way Zoe's eyes lit up as soon as we stepped inside of the lodge. Looking around this place, it was everything it was made out to be. Trees were in each corner of the room, and candles were burning on each of the tables in the center of a bowl decorated with scented pinecones. A Christmas-like aroma aroused my senses. Stockings hung from the tall fireplace that was burning adjacent to the table I presumed was set for us.

Sitting down at the table, I couldn't help but admire Zoe's beauty. The lodge was breathtaking and even more so because of the girl who was sitting right in front of me. When I heard about this place, I wasn't sure what to expect. Frankly, my nerves were getting the best of me. I heard an ad on the radio the other day about a "magical and romantic destination for the perfect date." It stemmed my curiosity because I had been thinking about planning another date for Zoe that entire day, so I had to check it out. From my observations thus far, this was more beautiful than I thought it would be.

The lodge was named "Lorraine's," a family owned restaurant. When I called to make reservations a week ago, I expected for them to ask me questions like "What's your name? Phone number? What time do you want your reservation for?"—all the same questions you normally got for every restaurant. Well, I got those, but they also continued to a series of strange questions.

"This is amazing. How did you find this place?" Zoe grinned.

"I have my ways. I'm glad you like it, Zoe." I smirked. I wasn't about to tell her I took a chance on something I didn't know about.

When we sat down, a man dressed as an elf approached us.

"Welcome to Lorraine's, where the magic of Christmas is celebrated all year long. Can I get you started with something to drink?"

The smile on Zoe's face said it all, and she let out a slight laugh. The place was different. It was unlike any other restaurant, and she seemed to love it. Now I understood why they described it as magical. It was February, but in here, it was still Christmas.

"I'll take a water."

"I'll have the same," I said after Zoe.

"This place is now my new favorite place ever," she said while looking around. "Seriously, where did you ever find it? I have lived here my entire life and I've never heard of it." Her eyes lit up while admiring all of the Christmas decor throughout the lodge. "And Christmas is my favorite time of year! How did you know?"

"I guess I just know you better than you think." Luck seemed to be on my side tonight, thankfully.

*

The night was going perfectly. The dinner was amazing, except we were talking so much that by the time I finished it, it had become cold. Our conversation never seemed to end. A young woman, also dressed as an elf, approached our table with bags in her hands.

"How are you enjoying your evening?" she asked cheerfully. I recognized her voice. She must have been the woman I spoke to on the phone.

"Great! This place is amazing!" Zoe spoke up right away and continued to rave about it to the woman.

"I have something for each of you. We want thank you for spending your night with us here at Lorraine's. We hope that you had a magical time!" She winked at me as she handed a bag to the both of us. I stared at the bag placed before me on the table, unsure of what it contained.

"What is this?" Zoe asked, laughing.

"I'm not sure. Should we open them?"

"You first." She said.

"Okay, okay." She was hard to argue with so I opened the bag first. Before I took out what was inside, I now know what those questions meant on the phone. It was a mini Bop It. I could feel the huge grin that was appearing on my face. I got nervous when I began to think—what was in Zoe's bag?

"Well?" Zoe asked curiously.

Pulling it out of the bag, I laughed. "It's what I've always wanted for Christmas! A Bop It!"

"Stop it. You've never had a Bop It?" Zoe glared at me. "I cannot wait for this! I am undefeated. I'm the master. Gabe's not so bad either!"

"Oh, are you? No one beats me at anything."

"Guess you will know what it feels like to lose then shortly."

"Well, what is in your bag? Open it." I was curious to see what was in her bag. This could potentially make or break the evening since she seemed so excited.

Gently taking the tissue paper out of the bag, she smiled, pulling out a light green scarf that brought out the beautiful color of her eyes. As she continued to dig deeper in the bag, her smile faded, and tears appeared in her eyes as she pulled out the second item.

"What's wrong?" She sat still, staring into the bag.

What else was in there? I got worried.

"This is beautiful. I don't understand. Did you do this? How did you do this? I've never seen this picture before."

"No, honestly I don't know what you're talking about." I was confused.

She pulled out a small snow globe and turned it to face me. Inside the snow globe was a picture. Tears trickled down her face, and I couldn't tell if they were happy tears or sad ones.

"Look." She smiled and handed me the snow globe from across the table. "This is a picture of my parents when they were younger."

How did they know? I looked around for the staff, but they were clearly letting us have a moment as they all seemed to have disappeared. Staring at the couple in the picture, I now realized how they probably knew. Zoe could have been her mother's twin. She was beautiful, just like her daughter. But it still didn't explain how they got their hands on this picture.

"They look so happy, don't they? My dad was so good to her. Can I see it again?"

"It looks like it was taken here," I said, handing it back to her, after I noticed that the fireplace they were standing in front of happened to be identical to the one adjacent to us.

"Wait, what?" She grabbed it from my hands abruptly. Staring at the fireplace and back at the picture, she was speechless. Silence remained between the both of us for a few moments until an older gentleman approached our table.

"Good evening! My name is Luciano. I am the owner here. How did you enjoy your evening?"

"It was amazing! Thank you so much for a wonderful time. You have a great place. I've never been anywhere like it," I said, shaking his hand.

"I loved it!" Zoe paused and looked down at the snow globe. "Did you know them?"

"Your parents, you mean? Yes, I did. They used to come here every year." Luciano replied.

"Really? I wonder why my mom never told me about this place," Zoe said.

"This picture is from their first time here. They were a bit younger than you, I presume. I had this made up for them way back when, but your father told me to keep it here. He said the first time he took your mother here was when he realized he was in love with her."

"How did you know who I was?" Zoe's voice was shaken up a bit. I, too, was in shock that this was all happening. The words that escaped from his mouth were powerful and left me with unfamiliar emotions.

"When you walked in through the door, I knew right then. You are the spitting image of your mother. I knew she had a daughter named Zoe, so when I heard this fine young man say your name, I didn't have a doubt."

"This means a lot. It really does. I don't even know how to thank you." Zoe stood up and gave him a hug, which took Luciano by surprise, but he welcomed it. By now even I had tears in my eyes. This was hard to wrap my head around.

"No need to thank me. I just hope you two will visit again soon."

"Oh, we will be! Where do we get our bill?" Christian asked. It was starting to get late, and we needed to head home even though neither of us wanted to leave.

"Don't worry about it," Luciano said quietly before smiling.

"Oh, wow. You didn't have to do that. You are so kind." I was floored.. Tonight couldn't have been any more unpredictable.

Standing up, I shook his hand, thanked him again, and I grabbed my coat as Zoe stood up to help put it on her. Taking her hand I led her toward the doorway. Walking down the steps into the snow, she stopped and pulled me closer to her, kissing me unexpectedly.

"Thank you so much. Tonight was amazing," she said while releasing her lips and staring into my eyes. We were out in the cold, but warmth filled my body as I took Zoe's hand. It seems that just as her father fell in love with her mother, I think I have fallen in love with Zoe at the very same place.

Zoe sat on the back of the snowmobile holding her helmet in her lap. The wind was starting to pick up as the night got colder. Her hair blew back behind her, and her smile glowed, bringing light to the dark skies.

"Well, are we going to leave?" she said as she smiled back at me. I hesitated to move. I just want to stand here for a minute longer. If I could freeze time and stay in one moment for the rest of my life, this would be it.

{21}

Zoe

I sat on the back of the snowmobile and waited for Christian to join me. Looking ahead, I saw an empty ice covered path lit up from the moon and the stars. Looking behind, the beautifully decorated lodge sat on a small hill, surrounded by snow covered pine trees, and lights illuminated the sidewalk. It was picturesque.

Christian peered out of the doorway and stopped at the top of the stairs right underneath the porch light. I looked at him, and there was nothing left to fear. The unspoken echoed loudly through the silence, awakening an invisible energy that connected our hearts, our souls. He made me feel alive again.

He finally hopped on the snowmobile and powered it up.

"Ok, I'm ready." I wrapped my arms around his waist.

"Wait, look up there!" He pointed up toward the sky.

"I don't see anything."

"Over there." My eyes followed in the direction of his left arm up over the trees toward the darkness and caught sight of the flame burning through the sky.

"Make a wish," Christian turned around and whispered in my ear. His warm breath hit my neck as he spoke, sending goose bumps down my arms. I rested my head on his back and closed my eyes gently and made a wish.

"What did you wish for?" he asked.

"If I tell you, it may never come true." I smiled.

"Alright, hold on tight."

I held him just as tight as I did on the way here. The only difference was that this time I wanted more.

We drove back along the path we took to get here. I envisioned what it would be like to know every part of him.

As he drove the snowmobile into the back of the trailer, I tapped Christian on the shoulder as he slowed down until coming to a complete stop.

"Everything okay?" he asked me.

"Yeah, but I have an idea." I grabbed my keys and headed toward my car.

"What's that?" He questioned.

"Follow me." I started up my car and waited until he got in his to start driving.

We drove for about ten miles until I pulled into the parking lot of a motel I had noticed on the way here. Christian parked next to me, and without asking any more questions, looked me in the eye and opened his door. He headed toward the office.

I leaned up against the hood of my car while I waited. I took a deep breath in and smiled as I watched the door open. As he slowly approached me, our eyes never lost contact. Reaching out for my hand, he led me to room 103.

He turned around quickly after opening the door and picked me up. My legs wrapped around his waist. Our foreheads touched, and we both smiled. He gently placed me down on the bed and walked over toward the door.

I watched as he turned the lock and rested against the back of the door. I grabbed the bottom of my shirt and slowly lifted it over my head. Christian turned around and I motioned with my pointer finger for him to come closer until he was standing right in front of me.

I placed my hands underneath his shirt and stood up as I slowly moved it up his body. I admired his abdominal muscles as his shirt rose above his chest, sliding up and over his head. Wrapping my arms around his neck, his hands moved up my back until reaching my bra straps, which he slid off of my shoulders and unclipped.

We slowly laid backward until his body was completely on top of mine. He gently brushed the hair out of my face and tucked the loose strands behind my ear.

"My God, you are beautiful," he whispered as he leaned forward until our lips met each other's once again. This time, it was different. There was a fire between us that continued to get hotter. He grabbed my hands and held them while lifting them up and over my head.

Time was lost in the dark of the night. Eight o'clock had become nine o'clock. I laid my head on his bare chest and listened to the beat of his heart. Neither of us spoke until my phone rang.

"I'll just let it go to voicemail." The phone stopped and the room was silent again.

It rang a second time. I reached over the side of the bed and into my jacket pocket.

"It's Emily." I looked at Christian in a panic.

{22}

Gabe

The game ended a while ago. Janice and I were watching movies the rest of the afternoon until she brought dinner to me. She made pulled pork and fries. It was so good. I was only able to eat a little bit of it, though, because I haven't been feeling well. My legs have been really weak today too. Sometimes I can barely move them out of my bed or up in the air. Zoe told me I shouldn't walk anywhere by myself when they feel like this.

"Will you be okay when I leave? Emily just got here."

"Really?"

"Yes, really, and if you need anything just have her call me! I am going downstairs. She should be here any minute. I'll see you tomorrow."

Janice gave me a kiss on my forehead before heading back downstairs. Emily was my sister's best friend. She has been coming over here for the last couple of years to hang out with me when Zoe had to work and Janice needed a break. I loved when she came over. She's really pretty.

I set my cup of water on my nightstand. I couldn't drink anymore. My head was starting to hurt now, and all I wanted to do was sleep. I had to try and stay awake to hang out with Emily for at least a little bit.

I laid my head down on the pillow and turned to face the doorway. My eyes were starting to shut, but I heard Emily heading up the stairs. Walking in my room, she had a present in her hand.

"Hey, buddy! What's up?" she said while handing me the bag. "I brought you a little something."

"You always do! What is it?"

"Open it and see!"

I tried to sit up in my bed, but I was struggling. "Can you open it for me?"

"Are you feeling okay?"

"I'm just really tired and really weak today. I don't think my muscles are working right."

Opening the bag, she took out a t-shirt. I smiled.

"This is one of the t-shirts we had made up for the game today that we were throwing out to the crowd. Shh—don't tell anyone I stole it just for you." Emily smirked.

"I want to wear it. Can I?"

"Yeah, obviously!" She lifted the shirt I was wearing up over my head. Sometimes I needed help getting dressed too.

"Oh, shoot, it still has the tag on it. Are there scissors up here?" she asked me and I laid my head back down.

"No, I don't think so," I said quietly.

"Okay, let me run downstairs quick and grab some. You okay?"

"Yeah."

A few minutes passed. Emily must not have been able to find the scissors. All of the water I drank really made me have to use the bathroom. I had to go so bad. If I didn't get up, I might wet the bed, and that would be *so* embarrassing. I tried yelling to Emily, but I didn't have the energy to yell. Maybe I can do it.

I can do this. It's only across the hallway.

I moved my legs to the side of my bed and pushed myself up. I put my one hand on my nightstand and the other on my bed. Standing on my feet, I looked out my door. I didn't want to let go of my bedside. The bathroom seemed so far away, but I couldn't hold it in any longer. It started to hurt I had to go so bad. Taking a few steps, I made it to my doorway before I had to stop and hold onto the side of the wall.

Putting one foot in front of the other, I reached with my right hand to grab onto the railing of the stairs. Standing against the side of the wall, I pushed myself forward. Only a few more steps. I looked down the stairs, and I could see Emily coming from around the corner.

"Gabe! What are you doing?" she yelled to me and started to run up the stairs.

All of the sudden my legs felt like they were going to break. I went to reach for the railing, but my head was spinning so it looked blurry. I started to see black.

{23}

Christian

The fate of the night had all changed. The happiness, excitement, and passion diminished. The look in Zoe's eyes after answering the phone call frightened me.

After hanging up with Emily, Zoe threw her clothes on within seconds. She was talking fast, suggesting that she would just call me with updates, but I couldn't let her do that. I couldn't leave her at a time like this when she would need me the most.

Following closely behind, I ignored her request to go home. I coasted along the roads going almost thirty miles per hour over the speed limit just so I could keep up with her. Fearing that the cops would be out tonight, my eyes continuously watched my rear view mirror for lights that may appear.

When we arrived at the hospital, Zoe took no time getting out of her car before she frantically ran to the entrance. I tried to catch up to her.

In the waiting room, Emily was pacing back and forth. As soon as she spotted us, she ran in our direction.

"I shouldn't have left him. I shouldn't have gone downstairs. I'm so sorry, Zoe. I'm so—"

Before Emily could finish, she broke down into tears as Zoe embraced her.

"It's not your fault. Where is he now? What happened?" Zoe replied as she let go of Emily and wiped away the tears from her eyes. Her face was swollen as if she had been crying for hours.

"I…I brought him one of the shirts from the game, and I went downstairs to find scissors to cut the tag off and then…then…ugh, Zoe, I'm so sorry. I was coming around the corner, and I saw him standing at the top of the stairs. I ran to him, but I was too late. He passed out and started to fall down the stairs." At this point Emily could hardly get the words out of her mouth. She was in a state of sheer panic. "I called 911 and then called Janice. She drove me here. She just went to the bathroom quick."

"Emily, listen to me. It's not your fault. He's been getting worse. He's hardly been eating, and this morning he couldn't even get out of bed." Zoe's voice was shaking. I took her hand, gripping it tight.

I know what it feels like to lose a brother, to lose your best friend. I can't imagine what it must feel like to think that you could lose the only person you had left. I wish there was something I could do right now that would make this all go away.

"Is there anything I can do?" I asked her.

Zoe turned to face me, grabbing my other hand.

"You are amazing. All we can do is wait right now while the doctors examine him. They're probably going to have to run tests as well, so it could be a while. You don't have to stay. You really don't. It could be a long night."

"But I want to." I kissed her. I wasn't going to leave her or Gabe.

*

An hour has passed, and the only new information we have is that the doctor said it shouldn't be much longer before Zoe can see him. *Thank God*, I thought to myself, looking around at all of the people we were surrounded by. I needed to go take a walk. It broke my heart to see Zoe suffering this much. I didn't want to tell her that I was growing weaker myself, so I offered to go grab coffee. That way I could get myself together.

On my way to find the cafeteria I passed the chapel. Pushing the doors open, I walked in and mindlessly sat down in a pew.

'James, if you can hear me, please give Gabe the strength he needs to get better. I wish you were here today to meet Zoe and Gabe. I've fallen in love with her. Surprised, right? Me? In love? I know. But this girl is amazing. She's selfless, strong, beautiful, and such an amazing sister to her brother. Gabe is sick, and he is the only family she has left. Right now he needs all the help he can get. I miss you every day, JJ. I love you. I didn't tell you that enough, or how much I appreciated everything you did for me."

Tears streamed down my face. This was all too familiar to me. I looked around and memories flooded my mind from the last time I sat in this very chapel. In the same exact pew, I sat back and closed my eyes. The door opened, interrupting my thoughts, and sent my body jolting.

"I'm sorry. I didn't mean to startle you," Emily whispered.

"You didn't. Sorry. I was just thinking."

"This is awful."

"I've been here before." I stared at the front of the chapel. "We were standing at the front, and we lit a candle, then sat in this very pew to pray. We prayed that James would have the strength to survive. I was terrified. I didn't know if I would ever see him again."

"James?" Emily questioned.

"My brother," I replied before continuing.

"At that young of an age, the silence was scaring me. I turned around and I noticed a girl who looked to be about my age sitting by herself near the back with her head downward. Her body was shaking. I got up and walked over to her, noticing that her lips were quivering. She looked just as alone and as scared as I was."

"How old were you?" Emily asked.

"Fourteen. She asked me why God did these things to us, why he put us in these situations. I didn't know what to say to her. I don't even know if now I would have had an answer. Water poured out of her eyes down her face, and in that moment I knew I wasn't alone in the world."

I teared up thinking about it.

"I never even learned that little girl's name. So much was going on, I never thought to ask her. But she gave me the strength to get through my brother's death because I knew then that I wasn't the only one dealing with loss. It helped me get through that tragic time, and I often found myself thinking of her."

"I'm sorry you had to go through all of that. I didn't know. I'm sorry." Emily's hands clasped and she leaned forward.

"It's okay. Not too many people know. Being here and seeing what Zoe's going through is hard. It brings back those memories, and it's hurting me to see her go through this."

"You really care about her, don't you?"

I nodded in agreement.

We headed back toward the waiting room with several cups of coffee in hand. I was anxious. Hopefully we would have answers soon. Coming around the corner I stood still and watched Zoe from the distance. Even at her worst, she was beautiful. I admired the way her strength and composure radiated off of her. The doctor came out and headed toward her. The floor seemed to disappear beneath my feet, and I had to brace myself up against the wall.

{24}

Zoe

My mother paced back and forth, hands over her head to open her airway when her breathing became difficult. I watched several patients being wheeled down the hallway to the surgical floor and the doctors scramble around to where they were supposed to be. My dad was hooked up to so many machines. It pained my mom to see him like that, so she wouldn't let me in the room. At the time I didn't understand why.

But I was thirteen. I was meddlesome. His doctor came over and asked to speak with my mother. She didn't want me to hear what kind of condition he was in, so she asked me to step aside. I did what any other kid would do. I disobeyed her orders and snuck around the corner. Quickly turning into my dad's room, I stood there confused and in shock.

How could this happen? He was so healthy, I thought to myself while approaching his bedside.

Slowly sitting down in the chair next to him, I didn't want to wake him, but he must have heard me because he turned his head and gently opened his eyes.

"Zoe?" When he spoke, his voice was hoarse.

"Yes, Daddy, I'm here. I'm here." I choked on my words.

"Where's your mother? Where's Gabe?"

"The neighbors are here watching Gabe in the waiting room. Mom's talking to the doctor right now."

"Zoe." He coughed. "I need you to listen to me. Tell your mother that I love her—"

"Daddy don't," I interrupted him and started to cry.

"Tell Gabe about me. Protect him like I always protected you. You will always be my baby girl, but when the time comes for prom wear a dress that makes you look like a princess. When you have your first boyfriend—" at this point he couldn't control his cough. I handed him the cup of ice that sat next to him. My hand shook inside of his and the tears filled up my eyes. I leaned into him and began to cry hysterically in his arms.

He continued, "...and many after that. Just make sure they treat you like I treat your mother, even better in fact. You deserve the best. You won't have to miss me because I'll always be with you."

"Don't leave me, Daddy. You can't leave mom and me and Gabe. You're going to get better. You'll see. The doctors will make you better. That's why you're in the hospital." I reached for a tissue to wipe my nose, but immediately relieved the pressure of my body on his chest and sat up when I noticed he was having trouble breathing.

"I love you Zo Zo. Don't ever—" His hand let go of mine and he grabbed his chest.

"Help! My Daddy needs help! Someone help me!" I screamed as loud as I could, so loud my throat started to hurt and I thought my head would explode. The doctors came running in. They tore off his hospital gown, revealing his bare chest, and shocked him. His body jolted upward in reaction. I slowly backed away, tripping over my feet. My eyes were glued to the sight of my entire world falling apart.

"Again!" the doctor yelled out.

A nurse pulled me out of the room, and I looked to my left to see my mom running. Grabbing me into her arms, she held me tight, and we watched through the window as the doctors tried to save his life. They continued to shock him, and the doctor pushed on his chest rapidly with an intense force.

Looking up, the doctor made eye contact with me through the window. I was only thirteen. I didn't know what was going on. All I knew was in that moment the doctor saw me, and as a result he continued to keep trying. But there was nothing more they could do, and all at once the doctors slowly backed away from his body. I could no longer see because the tears in my eyes blurred my vision. Everything around me seemed to be moving in slow motion. Words began to flow from my mom's mouth, but I don't know what she was saying. The only voice I could hear was my dad's. I played what he said to me over and over again in my head.

The doctor exited the room and stood to face us. Pulling his mask down to his chin, the words "I'm so sorry. We did everything we could" tore mine and my mother's hearts into shreds.

I hoped that a doctor would never have to say those words to me again.

*

Holding Gabe's hand while he slept, I couldn't escape the memories of my father's death. I looked out of the window in Gabe's hospital room and saw that Christian was still sitting there. His hand was holding his fallen head as he slept. Having Christian in my life at a time like this was a blessing. He's been there for me more than I ever expected he would be. Thinking about that scared me. It scared me because this was all new to me. Scared because it was a never-ending fear that he would leave just like everyone else has when things get too difficult.

Lifting my legs in the air, it took all of the energy I had to put both feet on the ground. Walking out into the hallway, I found a seat next to Christian. Grabbing his hand, I placed it in mine.

I gently kissed his cheek, and he awoke suddenly.

"How is he? Is he awake yet?"

"He's woken up a few times, but I told him to go back to sleep. He needs his rest, and I'm not going anywhere."

"Me either," he said looking me right in the eyes.

"You can leave. You don't need to stay. You need sleep."

"I want to be here for you and Gabe. It wouldn't even cross my mind to leave you at a time like this. I'm not leaving, and you can't make me." I looked toward the ground and watched as his other hand grabbed mine.

"Can't fight with that, I guess."

"I asked about Gabe, but Zoe, are you okay? Be honest."

"Yeah."

"Look at me."

"I can't."

"Look at me, Zoe."

I looked up and stared right into Christian's eyes. I could clearly see that he was just as scared as I was. Smiling, he reassured me once more that he wasn't going anywhere. He brushed my hair out of my face. My lips were starting to tremble. With pains present in my chest, it became hard to breathe. The tears built up in my eyes. Here it is. I've hit my breaking point.

"I can't do this. I can't be strong anymore. It's just too hard."

Christian pulled me in closer and didn't let go. The tears poured down my cheeks, forming wet marks on his shirt.

"Yes, you can. Babe, you are the strongest person I know. Everything is going to be okay. He's going to get better. He will get better."

"I'm not too sure about that."

"What do you mean? You told me the doctor said Gabe will be fine." He wiped the tears off of my cheek. I couldn't hide any more details from him. I needed to be honest.

"What's going on, Zoe? You told me the doctor said Gabe will be okay," he repeated himself.

"I lied." The words released gently off of my tongue.

"Talk to me. What's wrong?"

"He's getting worse, and he needs chemotherapy. We were lucky enough to be a part of a clinical trial to avoid the heavy costs of the treatments. Due to the severity of how much his cancer has advanced, I'm afraid we don't have much time anymore. If we don't get him started on chemo soon, the doctor told me it could be a year at the most."

I could barely breathe after the words slipped through my lips. It was the first time I was saying any of this out loud. It's the first time I have come to accept that I may only have a year left with my brother.

"He's so young. He's my only brother. My insurance won't cover it, and I have no money. I won't be able to finish school."

"There has to be something they can do, right?" Tears fell down his face when he spoke.

"No, there's not. Chemo is our last option. We've tried everything else. So it's the only way he will beat this. How am I...how am I going to tell Gabe? I can't tell him he's getting worse and that I can't afford to get him the treatment he needs to stay alive, that he's going to go through hell if he gets the chemo, but it's the only way he will get better. I can't tell him. It's going to kill me to keep this from him. Watching him go through this is going to destroy me. I don't know how much more suffering I can watch him go through."

"He knows you are doing everything you can for him. It's going to be okay. I promise. I'm not going anywhere. We will get through this, and I say "we" because you are not alone. He's going to beat this. We are in this together."

I looked up and saw the pain in his eyes. He kissed me softly on my forehead, and as a result, I was somehow able to find a smile through the aching pain in my heart.

"I love you." It was the first time he's said those three words to me.

{25}

Christian

I sat in the chair, and the nurse tied the elastic band around my lower bicep.

"Sorry, this will only pinch for a second."

I clenched my other fist and turned my head as the blood started to come out.

"So you're donating your bone marrow? That's so wonderful," the nurse asked.

"I'm hoping to. To one person specifically."

Dr. Sheehan was able to pull me aside when Zoe left to go to the bathroom. She sent me down to the lab to get tests done to see if I would be ready to donate. When Zoe got back she had asked me to go to her house to grab a few things, which gave me the perfect opportunity to sneak out and do this.

"We're halfway through. How are you feeling?" She asked.

"Halfway? How much blood do you need to draw." I was starting to feel lightheaded.

"About fifteen vials. Your blood is being tested to see if your white blood cell count is high enough, among other things."

"When will I know if it is?"

"Not for a few days."

"What if the tests come back and I'm not ready? What do we do then?"

"You're going to have to talk to the doctor about that." The nurse replied while untying the band from my arm.

"We're done." She took the needle out from my arm and held a cotton ball down where the needle was.

I tried to stand up, but my head was spinning.

"Here, sit down for a minute. I'll get you some juice."

"Can you get me a piece of paper and a pen too?" I had an idea.

"Sure." The nurse opened the curtain and headed down the hall.

Once I was finally able to leave, I made a quick exit toward my car, hoping that Zoe wouldn't see that I was still here. Pulling in her driveway, I grabbed the letter I had written and walked toward the front door. I just needed to find the proper place to leave it.

The strong stench of cleaning supplies awakened my sense of smell as soon as I opened the door. Janice must have come over earlier to clean for them. In her kitchen I noticed that her fridge was covered in magnets, but nothing was hanging from them.

"Perfect," I said aloud while attaching the letter to a magnet. I had no doubt she'd notice it there.

Heading up to Gabe's room, I had to catch myself on the railing as I slipped from the newly cleaned steps. Several pictures of him and Zoe were hanging along the stairway wall leading into his room. Neatly placed on his bookshelf was a picture Zoe had taken of the two of us from the first night I came over. I picked it up and held it in my hands; I had to sit down. My hands shook. Everything about this moment reminded me of James and the grief I felt after his death.

James and I shared a bathroom that connected our two rooms. In the months after his death, the tension in the house continued to rise. My mother became very overprotective and I couldn't take it anymore. She didn't want anyone going in his room;

she wanted it to be left just the way it was. I think she just couldn't bear the thought of him not being in there if she looked in.

One night after getting into a huge fight with her, I went in for the first time since he died. Opening his door, I stood there, frozen. Taking slow steps, one foot in front of the other, I walked around touching various items that meant a lot to him. Most of his things were in boxes. After we packed them into our car, they had a neighbor bring them back up to his room, but they left them unpacked. It caused them too much pain.

I wiped off the dust that had accumulated on James' trophies that lined an entire wall. He was an incredible runner and placed in almost any race he entered. As skinny as he was, James managed to pack on a decent amount of muscle, something I struggled for years to do. He had jugs of protein in one cardboard box along with the many other supplements he took. I noticed another box on his floor. I presume it contained a lot of his favorite things because he labeled it "Don't touch or open." So I did what any other little brother would do—I opened it without giving it any thought.

Inside the box was an Mariano Rivera autographed baseball, a few shot glasses, a poster for his wall—and then I spotted it. It was a picture of the two of us after I had just made the game- winning point for my team. 'Best Friends' was written in marker along the bottom of the frame in poor handwriting. I gave this to him as a birthday present that year. I'll never forget that moment in the picture. It was the day I know I made my older brother proud.

Staring at the picture of Gabe. I was enraged. I didn't want Zoe to feel the same pain I felt after losing my brother. I didn't want her to feel it for a second time. It wouldn't be fair to her.

Sitting down on Gabe's bed, I couldn't hold it in any longer. Lying down, I wished and prayed for Gabe to get better and let all of the tears out that I was holding back. Turning over onto my side, the water in my eyes blurred my vision, but there was something through the blurriness that caught my attention.

I used my shirt to dab my eyes and wipe away the tears so I could see clearly. Standing up I walked over toward the wall and stood in front of the picture. I reached out and slowly placed my hand next to the frame. I had to brace myself. My heart was beating so fast I thought it was going to explode.

This couldn't be real, but I looked at the picture again and again and again.

How was this possible?

{26}

Zoe

"Gabe, can I interrupt you for a minute to talk?" The sadness in my voice alarmed him. He placed his book down and turned his head toward me.

"Can you get me some water?" I heard a weakness in his voice for the first time.

With my back turned toward him, I started filling up his cup. I stared at the wall and tried to put myself together before talking to him. Dr. Sheehan said it was important for me to be strong around Gabe. Lost in thought, the water spilled all over my hand.

"Here you go." I handed to him with a shaky hand.

"Thanks." He took a big gulp. "What do you want to talk about?"

"Well…" I moved closer and reached for his hand.

"What's wrong Zoe?"

"Your tests came back. Dr. Sheehan wants you to try a new treatment." The words quickly rolled off of my tongue out of nervousness.

"Another new treatment? Am I getting worse?"

"No," I lied to spare him the pain, "it's just that Dr. Sheehan found a better way to end your sickness. She thinks that this will be the last treatment you will ever have to do."

"If it doesn't work, am I going up to heaven to see Daddy?" His eyes widencd and he stared at me looking for answers. My heart ached at the panic in his voice.

"It's going to work. Dr. Sheehan has faith that it—"

He interrupted me. "Zoe, don't lie to me. I'm old enough to hear the truth. Am I dying?"

It took all I had not to cry.

"If we run out of treatments, the cancer could get worse. Then the angels of heaven will take you to see Daddy when God says it's time."

"But Zoe, I don't want to leave you. I'll miss you too much." Gabe started to cry and reached for me.

I got in bed and laid next to him, holding onto him tight. He laid his head down on my chest, and I couldn't hold it in any longer.

"You won't leave me. I promise. You are going to fight this."

"Will the new treatment hurt? I don't want to be in any more pain."

"I'm going to be with you every step of the way. Dr. Sheehan said you might feel sick with it, but then it gets better, and then the cancer will go away."

"Promise?" He held out his pinky.

I wrapped my pinky finger around his. "Promise."

*

Slamming her books down on the table and pulling out a chair, Emily's abrupt entrance nearly threw me out of my chair.

"Damn it, you nearly scared the shit out of me!" I yelled. The people sitting behind us motioned for us to be quiet.

"Well, wake up so we can get this done so you can get back to Gabe quicker. How is he doing today?"

"Can we not talk about how sick my brother is for once?" I looked outside at the gloomy day.

"Wow, sorry. Do you still want me to help you then, or should I just...go?"

"I'm sorry. I didn't mean to sound so bitchy. I told him today about how he had to get chemo. It was close to the worst conversation I've ever had to have."

"Oh Zoe, I'm so sorry."

"I just wish I could help him. I wish I could take away some of his pain away."

"I know, but the doctor seemed optimistic that this would work, right? Just try to stay positive! By the way, I talked to my parents."

"Stop. I told you not—"

"They mailed me a check. It's not that much, but you can put it toward his chemo treatments. Zoe, he needs it, and this isn't pity money. You are my best friend. We want to help you." She handed me the envelope from across the table.

"I really don't know what to say. Thank you. I don't know what I would do without you."

"Alright, where did we leave off? I think we are on part two of the paper, right?"

"Yeah, I think we can finish the whole thing today if we split it up." Emily and I had a very similar writing style, so she offered to write part of my paper as well to take a load off for me.

*

Two hours had gone by, and we weren't any closer to finishing it than we were when we got here. I tried to focus all of my attention on this, but I couldn't stop thinking about Gabe. Shockingly, Christian hardly even crossed my mind. On top of it all, I thought my stomach was going to eat itself from the inside out.

"I am so hungry I can't remember the last thing I ate."

"Zoe! You need to eat. Why haven't you been eating?" Emily scolded me.

"I don't know; with everything that happened today I just forgot. I haven't really had an appetite up until now."

"Alright, that's it. I'm going to go get us food. You stay here and finish this section. Do you want your usual?"

"I guess so." I leaned my head against my arm. I was starting to get a headache from lack of food.

"I'm getting you double. You need to eat!"

Emily took off, and I found myself putting aside my project again. I watched the rain hit the windows and the sky turn from gray to black. It was honestly miserable outside, and the weather made it even harder to get work done.

It didn't feel like winter. It felt more like a gloomy fall day. Cold, rainy, and dark. On days like today, all I wanted to do was wrap myself up in my bed, cry, and sleep. I never allowed myself to do so because I had to be so strong for everyone else around me. If I cried like that, I may never be able to stop.

Looking at my phone, I noticed that Emily's been gone for an awfully long time, longer than usual for a Sunday evening. But just then, she came around the corner. Her hood was up over her head protecting her hair from getting wet. Setting the wet plastic containers down on the table, she stood there as if she saw a ghost.

"What's the matter with you?"

Emily sat down and put her hand over her mouth.

"I don't know how to tell you this. I need to tell you something." She couldn't look me in the eye. She tilted her head down, looked back up at me, and proceeded to stare out the window.

"What happened Emily? You're scaring me. Just say it."

"I don't know. It sounds really bad. Really, really bad. It may not even be anything. I don't know."

I finally got her to spit it out. She continued to tell me what happened, and the thoughts in my head overpowered her voice. I turned to face the window, watching the rain hit harder against the glass. Closing my notebook, I threw it into my bag and put my hood up. Quickly getting up from the table, I ran out of the library, almost knocking someone's books off of their table. I barely missed running into someone.

"Zoe, wait!" Emily yelled. I heard her coming from behind me as I ran off.

I began to mindlessly run so fast that my hood couldn't stay up over my head. I had to see for myself. Loud claps of thunder roared, and lightning lit up the sky. I stared through the window, and when I thought my life couldn't get any worse, it had.

I didn't want to believe it. I thought I was seeing things, but I watched as he sat there laughing and smiling. I thought he only looked at me that way, but seeing the way he smiled and stared into her eyes as she talked, I was wrong. I was very, very wrong. I felt so deceived and cheated. Standing up from the table, they gave each other a hug, and I realized I had been there a moment too long.

Running and not turning back, I heard the door fly open, slamming loudly against the brick walls on the building.

"Zoe, hold up!" he yelled from behind me.

Sharp pains became present in my side, and I had to stop and catch my breath. I couldn't run any longer. The pain had become too much to handle.

"Zoe, I can explain!"

Turning around, I didn't care that the mascara had run all down my face and that my hair was soaking wet. I looked him in the eye and I wanted him to see how much more pain he had just put me in.

"Explain what, exactly? You lied to me. You lied to me, Christian. You told me you were going to be with your team today. You can't explain what I just saw. You were with Lacey, Lacey who happens to be your ex-girlfriend. I know what I was seeing. You lied to me. Of all days, I don't need this today."

"No, you don't, Zo. It's not what it looks like. It's really not." Christian's voice became weak as he reached for my hand, but I pushed it away and stepped back slightly.

"Then what were you doing with her? I needed you today. That's why I asked what you were up to. I needed you!"

The rain fell down from the sky harder. At this point I was completely soaked.

"I can't tell you what I was doing with her. Is everything okay?" He sighed.

"Oh, that just makes it so much better! Don't lie to me anymore, Christian. Just don't. I should have known. You didn't have to tell me you would be there for me if you didn't want to be just because you thought it would make me feel better. Lacey has it all. I get it. She has no baggage like I do. I can't deal with this anymore. I can't be put in any more pain."

"But Zoe…" Christian started to cry. But I couldn't stand here and hear any more of the lies or the bullshit.

"Just leave us alone. I don't need this. Not now. Bye, Christian."

I ran again until I got to my car, where I couldn't hold any more of it in. After everything, he had me convinced that he was different. But watching him sit there with Lacey, I've seen that look on his face before. He was happy. Seeing him sit there talking to her with that wide smile across his face hurt. It felt like my entire world came crashing down today.

{27}

Christian

"Are you coming?" Matt held the door open to the locker room.

"Give me a minute. I'll be right out." I wanted to take my jersey off. For the first time in my life, I didn't want to step out onto the court.

"You better hurry. Coach is gonna be pissed."

The door shut behind him. I reached into my bag and grabbed my phone. I was hoping to see a text from Zoe, wishing me good luck in today's game. There was nothing.

"Agh!" I angrily threw my phone across the room. It bounced off the wall onto the floor.

"God damn it!" I picked up my phone to find the entire screen shattered.

Pacing back and forth, I tried to calm down. I was irritated at myself. All I wanted to do right now was to go to the hospital and make things right with Zoe, but I couldn't. I couldn't tell her the truth, and that made this even worse.

I stood out on the court and tried to erase her from my memory so I could concentrate on the game. I tried, but it didn't work. The whistle blew, and I missed the ball as it was passed to me.

Five seconds into the game and I already had the ball stolen.

I could hear her voice inside my head saying "You lied to me, Christian. You lied to me." The voice continued to speak louder than all of the noise in the arena. The pain in her eyes and the sadness in her voice will never leave me.

*

I threw my sneakers across the locker room when I sat down. Losing today's game just made things even worse. The guys walked in slowly, and no one said a word until Matthew walked in and sat next to me.

"Michaels, what the fuck is your problem today, man? Where the hell were you out there? Way to blow the game for us."

"Leave me alone."

"Just saying. We needed you out there today, and you played like shit." He untied his sneakers.

"I said leave me alone, Matt."

"Don't tell me Zoe broke up with you. Aw, guys, I think Chris has a broken heart. Maybe we should all sit here and cry with him next time instead of picking up his slack on the court."

I tried to contain myself. I tried not to look at him. He was just pissed we lost. *Don't do anything stupid, Christian. Don't do it.* I put my hands on my knees and repeated to myself.

I could see out of the corner of my eye that a few of the guys were staring at me. Matt turned to the guy next to him and whispered something.

"What did you just say?" I spoke softly.

Matt didn't answer but the other guys continued to laugh.

"I said what did you say?" I picked my head up and stared at him waiting for a reply.

"He said—" One of the freshmen started to respond.

"I want to hear it from Matt."

"I said I bet Zoe wasn't satisfied but that I could show her a good time."

The blood rushed through my body faster than it ever had before. I couldn't stop myself. My fist left my lap as I stood up and flew across his face. Then on the ground, I found myself on top of him, hitting him so hard that blood flowed out of his nose. Our teammates came running and grabbed me off of him.

"Whoa, Chris, easy. Calm down." A few of my teammates held me back. I stared Matt in the eyes until I broke down. It wasn't just Zoe that was bothering me. It was everything that had been piling up over the course of the last few days. All of it was just too much for me to handle. I've never gotten physical with anyone before, especially one of my best friends. I stood up and punched the wall.

"You two with me *now!*" Coach Higgins walked in and pointed at Matt and I.

The team watched as we awkwardly made our exit out of the locker room.

"We are adults. We respect each other. We are a *team*. Now what happened?"

Neither Matt nor I spoke up.

"If neither of you are going to talk, you leave me no choice. You're both suspended from the next game."

"You can't do that!"

"I'm the coach. I can do what I want." Coach Higgins walked away.

"Don't suspend Matt. I started it. I hit him first," I admitted.

"Okay. Michaels, I want to see you in my office tomorrow."

I felt too guilty to let my anger be the cause of Matt getting in trouble. I was furious with Matt, but he was still my friend.

*

The bus home was even longer than the way there. I sat in the back by myself. Hardly anyone on the team was speaking to me. Not only did I blow the game for us today, but now I was suspended during our next game.

When we walked off of the bus, and no one said a word. Matt got a ride back to the townhouses with someone else. The house tonight was going to be awkward.

I got out of my car and walked through the path to my house. Someone was standing outside of my door, but it was too dark to see who it was. I could only make out a female figure

Maybe it's Zoe?

As I approached, I soon realized who it was.

"You need to leave. Now," I demanded and signaled for her to start walking.

"What's your problem?"

"You shouldn't be here." I snuck by her to open the door to my townhouse.

"I wanted to see if you were okay, after yesterday and all."

"Lacey, not now. Please leave."

"Are you going to tell her?"

"If she ever speaks to me again. Every minute that goes by, knowing how angry she is at me, feeling so deceived, it's painful."

"If you tell her it'll ruin it, Chris."

"Are we doing the right thing?" I questioned myself.

"Yes. Zoe will understand when the time comes."

"I can't wait that long for her to find out. I can't wait that long to talk to her." I was really missing talking to Zoe. I loved the sound of her voice and the way she made me laugh.

"Yes, you can. I know you can. Just focus on school and basketball." Lacey tried to console me. "Have you told your parents yet?"

"I'm going to call them tomorrow."

"I'm glad we can be friends, Chris. You know, after everything. I'm happy you asked me to help you."

"Me too. Thank you, but seriously, you need to go. I can't have you here."

"Understandable. Have a good night."

I said goodbye to Lacey and shut the door behind me. Matt was sitting in the kitchen with ice on his eye.

"Did I really hit you that hard?" I tried to laugh it off, but he just ignored me and walked upstairs.

First Zoe won't speak to me, and now my best friend. I feel like a terrible human being.

{28}

Gabe

"What are you doing here?" I asked as Christian walked in my room.

"I came to see how you were doing! It's been a while!" he replied.

"I'm confused." I tried to remember what Zoe told me her reason was for Christian not coming to visit me anymore. I've been in the hospital for three weeks now and he hasn't come once.

"What are you confused about? Wow, you really made it feel like home in here." He looked around at all of the decorations that my nurse and Zoe put up.

"Yeah, my nurse Danielle and Zoe put up a lot of the things from my room at home. But Zoe said something about you not coming to see me anymore."

"Oh, she did?" He looked sad as he sat down.

"Yeah, and she didn't tell me you were coming."

"She doesn't know I'm here. Can you keep that a secret?"

I thought about it for a minute. Something was going on with my sister and him, and Zoe wouldn't tell me the truth.

"Why? Why can't she know you're here?"

"Well, because she might get mad that I ditched our plans to come see you." I could tell that Christian was lying now too. I don't know why neither of them will tell me why. I'm old enough to know.

"Okay, I'll keep your secret. But on one condition." If he really didn't want me to tell Zoe I might be able to get something out of it.

"Oh, really? What's that?" Christian laughed.

"I want to go to your last game." I stared at him waiting for his reply.

"That's not really up to me."

"I know. It was worth a try. I really, really, really do want to go."

"I know you do. I'll tell you what. I'll see what I can do, but no promises."

"That works for me."

"Good," Christian replied.

I scratched my head, and a clump of hair came out. It started happening the other day and freaked me out. Dr. Sheehan said this was going to happen after I began my new treatment. Christian saw this and looked sad.

"The doctor said this was normal." I tried to cheer him up.

"How are you feeling?"

"I get really sick from this new treatment. I actually feel a lot worse. But Zoe says it's going to make me feel better, so I believe her."

"I know you'll get better too."

"Me too. Zoe hates seeing my hair come out, though. I think that makes her even more sad."

"She's been upset?" He looked concerned.

I took a sip of the water that was next to my bed.

"Yeah, and I really hate seeing her sad. I noticed that the only time she's happy is when you are around."

"Is that so?" Christian smiled.

"Yeah, but me too. I mean, it really makes me happy when you come and hang out with me too."

"Don't tell Zoe, but I enjoy hanging out with you more than her." He winked at me and we both laughed.

"Oh no." Tears poured out of my eyes and my hand covered my mouth. Christian grabbed the basket next to my bed and held it under my head as I sat up and leaned forward.

He helped walk me to the bathroom and sat on the floor with me while I got sick.

"I'm scared." I leaned against the toilet and held my hand to my stomach.

"I'm right here. I'm not going anywhere."

{29}

Christian

"Please don't go," Gabe pleaded.

"I won't."

"Promise?" he whispered.

"I promise."

"Are you going to come back to visit again soon?"

"I will try to!" I was excited. After how slow the last few weeks have gone by, finally, the night I've been waiting for is approaching. Gabe was going to get one big surprise.

"Can you come in two days?"

"What's in two days?" I bit my lip out of nervousness. Two days was the day I had a surprise planned for him, the day I've been planning for the last few weeks. I couldn't slip up.

"My birthday!" He exclaimed.

"Is it really?" I was shocked. I had no idea it was also his birthday. This was going to make the night even better. This was perfect.

"Yeah! I know it's your last home game, though, but if you could try…"

"I'll try my best!"

"Even though Zoe will be here?"

"Yes, even though Zoe will be here."

"Okay, good. Do you think you're going to win the game?"

"I think we have a good shot! Then we're onto the MAAC tournament!"

"I really hope you guys win that. That would be awesome!"

"Especially since it's my last year." It was really sinking in that there were only a few games left before my basketball career was over.

"I'm really going to miss seeing you play. Siena basketball won't be the same."

"I'm going to miss it too."

Gabe looked exhausted. He could hardly keep his eyes open. Getting sick seemed to take a lot out of him. You could see in his face that he's lost a few pounds since I've seen him last.

A loud vibration interrupted the silence of the room. Gabe's phone lit up on the table next to him. He lifted his arm to try and reach it, but seemed to be too weak to move. The look of struggle on his face broke my heart.

Getting up out of the chair, I walked around his bed to grab his phone for him. Looking down at the screen, I didn't know how to react.

"It's your sister." I handed him the phone, but it dropped out of his hand onto his bed.

"Can you put it on speaker? I can't hold it."

"Hey, buddy. How's your day going?" She spoke and I smiled at the sound of her voice.

"When are you going to be here?" Gabe asked.

"Five to ten minutes. I'm on my way now." Gabe looked at me. I needed to get out of here as soon as possible so she didn't see me.

"Can you stop and get me ice cream? I don't like what they have here at the cafeteria."

"Sure, I can do that. See you soon."

I hung up the phone for Gabe.

"How's she doing?" I asked curiously.

"Busy. She sleeps over there." He pointed to the cot in the corner of the room. "She never goes home."

It upset me to see what they were dealing with. She's been living in the hospital with Gabe. I thought of my letter. I had wondered if she saw it yet.

"She's a good sister!"

"The best!" he replied.

"Alright, I have to go!"

"I know. That's why I asked for her to stop at the store." Gabe smiled.

"You are very smart for an eight year old, you know that?"

"I'm almost nine now! I'll see you soon, right?"

"Yes, you will." I gave him a high five and grabbed my jacket from the chair. I was on my way out of his room before he stopped me.

"Wait!" Gabe yelled.

"Did I forget something?" I looked around the room.

"Just hold on."

Gabe uncovered himself and propped himself up in bed. Throwing his legs over the side of the bed he set one foot down at a time. His right hand held onto the side of the bed as he walked closer toward me.

"Be careful!" I ran over toward him.

I knelt down in front of him, and my hands grabbed his arms. His eyelids were blinking fast while his mouth twitched. This was the first time I've ever seen Gabe genuinely upset.

"Gabe, what's wrong?"

He threw his arms around my neck and started to cry.

"It's just I really missed you."

"Oh, Gabe, I missed you too."

"I love you, Christian."

I closed my eyes and tried to hold back my tears, but it was impossible not to cry. For the first time in a long time, it felt like I had a brother again.

"I love you too, Gabe."

*

I sat on my bed and stared at the unopened box on my desk. Most days I just glanced at it. Some days I forgot it was even there. But today, the temptation to open it was higher than it ever had been before.

I had found this box in James' room after his death. It was addressed to me. I never had the courage to open it before, but today I missed my brother more than ever.

Grabbing it from the desk, I carefully unwrapped the paper with my shaking hands. Taking the top off of the box and setting it to the side, I picked up the item that was placed underneath some tissue paper. It was a gold cross on a chain. Flipping it over, there was an engraving on the back of the cross, which read, *I can do all things through Christ who strengthens me. Philippians 4:13.*

Unhooking the clip, I placed the chain around my neck. I felt connected to him even though it was just a necklace. It was a reminder that even though James is gone, he will always be with me. Just those simple words remind me that God doesn't give anyone anything that they can't handle.

{30}

Zoe

By the time I got to the hospital, Gabe was asleep. One of the nurses let me put the ice cream in the freezer until after he woke up. He looked much worse than when I had left this morning. It broke my heart.

"Hey, can I borrow you for a minute?" Dr. Sheehan poked her head in the room.

I followed her into her office, and my nerves were getting the best of me. Having to go through the worst part of Gabe's sickness alone has been extremely difficult.

"Is he okay?" The worst possible scenarios were filling up my head

"It's still early to tell, but I think that this is going to work." Dr. Sheehan said reassuring me. I let out a sigh of relief.

"You're positive? How do you know?" I didn't want false hope.

"I really think so. But you're going to need to meet with the accounts department soon. I can only prolong this so long. Have you thought anymore about what you are going to do?"

"I know that there's not much more you can do. I'm almost done with school, though, and I'm going to take on another job and possibly take out a loan as well."

"I've been reaching out to different foundations too."

"Oh, you didn't have to do that." I was feeling helpless.

"You have so much going on; you shouldn't have to worry about it. I'm hoping I'll hear back soon, but your brother is a real fighter."

"He really is." I silently thanked God. I feared what would happen if he was to give up.

I left her office and headed down the hallway toward Gabe's room. I heard laughter and a few voices.

"Well, hello there! What is your name?" A boy who appeared to be a few years younger than Gabe sat next to his bed in a wheelchair. He wore a hat and was hooked up to an IV.

"My name is Johnny!"

"Hi, Johnny! My name is Zoe. I'm Gabe's sister. It's nice to meet you!" I shook his cold hand.

"What are you guys up to? I heard you laughing from down the hall!"

"We can't tell you that." Gabe looked happy to be with someone his age.

"I brought one of our new patients, Johnny, to come and meet Gabe. I thought they would enjoy spending time together!" Gabe's nurse Danielle came back into the room.

"Thank you," I turned my back away from Gabe and mouthed to her silently.

"Zoe, can I shave my head like he did?" Gabe asked, and Johnny removed his hat.

I looked over to Danielle.

"It might be time. His hair is falling out at a more rapid pace. He'll be more comfortable."

"If you really want to do that now, I guess we can."

"Look!" Gabe pulled a chunk of hair out, and he and Johnny laughed.

"I guess so. We need to get a razor."

"We have one here. I'll go grab it." Danielle quickly exited the room.

"I was just telling Johnny about the game tomorrow and how you get to go. He's going to ask his mom if he can come watch it in here with me."

"Oh, that's great. I'm sorry I have to work," I replied before getting lost in my thoughts. Tomorrow was senior night, the night they were recognizing Christian. I had no choice but to work, especially since I've called out from every game since my fight with Christian.

I felt bad about having to work. Tomorrow was Gabe's birthday. I told Gabe I would throw him a party this weekend since I can't tomorrow night. He was more than okay with it since he wanted to watch the game.

"I have everything you need right here." Danielle walked into the room with a head shaving kit. Handing it to me, I looked at Gabe, who looked nervous..

"I don't know if I could do it. Can you? Gabe, do you mind if Danielle does it? She would probably do a better job." The truth was that I was just scared.

She nodded and took the kit back from me.

"Here, let's go in the bathroom and do it." Helping him into a wheelchair, she wheeled him into the bathroom and shut the door behind her.

The buzzing sound made me cringe. I was nervous. I never thought it was going to get this bad. I just wanted Gabe to have a normal childhood.

"Is Gabe sick just like I am?" Johnny tugged at my shirt.

"Yes, he is. How old are you, Johnny?"

"I'm five." He held up one hand.

Five. Five years old, and Gabe was eight. My heart ached for the two of them.

"Wow!"

"Yup! My mom tells me I'm a big kid now, and since I'm a big kid I'm strong!" He punched his fists down and flexed like the Hulk.

I laughed in response. He was very animated, just like Gabe.

"Are your parents here with you?"

"Yeah, but they went home to grab some clothes. I'm in that room." He pointed to the wall behind us.

"Oh, cool! I'm glad Gabe has a friend like you to play with!"

"Me too."

The buzzing stopped and the bathroom door opened. Danielle wheeled Gabe out into the room.

"Well, what do you think?" He smiled and rubbed his hand on his newly shaved head.

"I think you look so handsome! I'm proud of you, buddy!" I stood there and watched my little brother look at himself in the mirror. I could see the pain and sadness all over his face.

*

Walking into the quiet house, I walked straight upstairs. Gabe asked me to get a few hats for him to wear so his head wouldn't get cold.

"Ugh, where is it?" I said aloud while digging through his bin of hats. He specifically requested his green Siena winter hat.

I walked into the bathroom and stared at my shower. Grabbing a clean towel, I stripped myself of my clothes and turned on the hot water. After staying in the hospital for so long, it felt nice to take a shower in the comfort of my own home.

Before heading back to the hospital, I chose to selfishly take some time to myself. Walking down to the kitchen, I decided to make myself a cup of chamomile tea and just take a few moments to relax. Sitting on the counter waiting for the water in my teapot to heat up, I caught a glimpse of something that I've never noticed before. My eyes were glued to the fridge. There was something hanging by a magnet screaming for me to grab it.

I jumped down and stood there staring at it before ripping it off. I put my finger under the right corner to tear it open, but my tea kettle whistled.

I didn't realize that my hands were shaking until I poured myself a cup of tea. My unsteady hand knocked into my cup, spilling some of the hot water all over the counter. Cleaning it up and pouring myself another cup, I brought the mysterious envelope into the other room with me. I sat on the couch and held it up to the light to see if I could make out anything that was on the inside. It was a letter.

My hands hadn't stopped shaking, so I tried to rip it open without ripping what the envelope contained. I sat back and took a deep breath.

Unfolding the piece of paper, tears filled my eyes once I had recognized whom it was from. I flipped it over and closed my eyes. I couldn't bring myself to read it.

How long has this been on my fridge? I wondered to myself.

I took another deep breath, and my eyes moved from left to right across the paper.

Dear Zoe,

I sit here tonight not even knowing where to start, but I'm going to start by thanking you. You have been the greatest gift God's given me. I didn't know I could love someone as much as I love you.

From the very moment we bumped into each other and I knocked that red cup out of your hands, I couldn't forget you. You were so beautiful, and I had to find you again. You had become a permanent presence on my mind, and I didn't even know your name. I knew that moment that you were the one. Wow. I can't believe I am even saying that. But it's true.

I'm so proud of the amazing woman you are. I love the way you call me Christian instead of Chris. I love the way your eyes light up every time Gabe laughs. The amount of strength and courage you have is honestly more than I could have. You are an inspiration and are doing such a great thing for Gabe. I am very happy to be a part of your life, and when he gets rid of this horrible sickness, which he will, I have so much planned for the both of us.

I've been thinking a lot lately about the future, and…well… I don't know what it holds for us, but I know it has to be something great. I believe that God placed us in each other's lives for a reason, and now I can't imagine my life without you in it. I love you so much.

Just know I will always be there for you.
Always.

I love you Zo.
Christian

Folding up the letter, I placed it on the table in front of me. Re-reading it one last time, I picked up my phone. But I couldn't do it. I couldn't bring myself to call him right now.

He was the love of my life too. Maybe he was right. Maybe he really couldn't tell me why he was with Lacey. It still didn't make sense to me, but I had to have a little faith, I guess. I needed to trust him. Now I have to talk to him at the game tomorrow. I hope it's not too late to fix things.

"Oh my God," I said out loud. "What did I do?"

{31}

Zoe

I slipped the green pullover on over my head. Zipping up my khaki pants, I bent down to put my leggings away in my backpack and pulled on my brown boots. Opening the door to the bathroom, I wandered out into the dark hallway. People were just starting to come into the arena to get it set up for the game.

"I read the letter. I love you too." I recited aloud what I wanted to say to Christian when I saw him.

"The letter you wrote was beautiful."

I don't know what to say. I sighed.

Approaching the main entrance, I spotted my boss carrying a big box. I quickly picked up my pace and opened the door for her.

"Thanks, Zoe!"

"No problem. That was perfect timing. New giveaways today?"

"Yeah, new shirts we're giving out."

"Oh, really? Can I see them?" I loved getting the free shirts so I could give them to Gabe.

"They're all wrapped up. I have to count them still. I'll get you one later. Thank you for coming in early today!" She shuffled to keep the box closed as she spoke. "So today I want you to…" I zoned out. I didn't want to come in early today. I hated that I wasn't spending the night with Gabe.

"I'm sorry, what did you say? Social media again?" I questioned confidently.

"Zoe, I had to pull you from that since you weren't here the last few games. You're going to be receptionist today."

I looked past the curtain that was behind my boss, and my eyes drifted to the empty court.

"Do I have to? Can I do something else? I want to be able to watch the game."

"I'm sorry. I already have the assignments written out, and you need to be up there in a few minutes. Nobody else is here to start answering the phones."

"Since when do we have someone answering—"

"Since today," she quickly interrupted me. "You'll have to think about that next time you call out of a game…or a few."

I couldn't even back myself up. I had no excuse. I called out because I didn't want to see Christian. Now, today, I wanted to see him more than ever, and I wouldn't get a chance to. This was just my luck. This would happen.

I took the long way around the arena to get to the office. I tried to prolong it as long as I could. I checked the time on my phone. If I walked slow enough, I'd see the team walk into their locker room. So I slowed down my pace…a lot.

I looked behind me and again ahead of me. No sign of my boss. I slowly turned around and headed back in the opposite direction. Then I turned back around again.

Coming around the corner, the door up ahead swung open. I stood to the side behind a vending machine so no one would see me. I peeked my head out and watched as the team walked in wearing their warm ups with their bags in hand. After each person I waited and waited, but there was no sign of Christian.

I waited a few minutes after the last person walked in, hoping that Christian was just late off of the bus. But he never came.

I couldn't have missed him. I started to second-guess myself.

Step by step up the stairs, I made my way to the office. Turning on the light, I looked around. All the desks were empty. People were walking by on their way into the arena. I looked at the empty chair at the reception desk.

Sitting down, I spun around. Leaning back, I looked up at the ceiling and sighed.

Tonight was going to suck.

{32}

Gabe

"Happy birthday!" Danielle yelled while walking into my room.

"Thank you!" I'm so excited. Today is going to be awesome. I just know it will be.

"Here, open it!" She handed me a present wrapped in green paper.

I tore off the wrapper paper like it was Christmas morning and stared at the box.

"What is it?" I asked.

"Open it and see!" Johnny said. He sat next to me and was just as happy. It was nice to have a friend who also had cancer.

I took the top of the box off and felt the soft green blanket.

"It's so comfy! Thank you!"

"You didn't see the best part. Here, look."

She took the blanket out of the box and held it open.

"A Siena blanket? Wow! Thank you!"

"That's so cool!" Johnny felt how soft it was.

She laid it across my bed. It matches perfectly with the new basketball pillows that Zoe gave me. She got me that and a few books

I wanted.

I'm jealous that she is going to be at the game today. Today was senior day, which means that it's Chris's last game ever!

"Danielle?"

"Yes, Gabe?"

"I can still watch the game tonight, right? I can't miss this one. It's Chris's last regular season game and Johnny and I wanna watch it!"

"Don't worry. Yes, you can!"

"I made sure Janice brought my shirt so I could wear it today while I watched the game."

"That was nice of her!" Danielle said back while getting my medicine ready.

"Yeah. I didn't put it on until after Zoe left, though. I didn't want to hurt her feelings. She's been so sad ever since Chris stopped coming around." I sighed.

"Did you ever find out what happened?" Danielle asked. I sometimes talked to her about it.

"No, I didn't. They both lied to me. But I want them to get back together because they're happier that way."

"You are a very smart kid! I hope so too. He seems like a really nice guy."

"He is," I replied, but my eyes were too heavy for me to keep them open.

"Can you turn off the lights? I think I'm going to take a nap," I asked and covered myself with my new blanket.

"Bye Gabe! See you later!" Johnny waved goodbye while walking out the door with Danielle.

*

"Sorry to wake you, buddy. You need to get ready," Danielle said. I was in the middle of a really good dream when she came in.

"For what? You told me I didn't have chemo today!" I was a little confused and still waking up, so I instantly got upset.

"Nope, you're right; you don't. But there's a huge surprise waiting for you."

"What is it?" I sat up so quickly I got dizzy.

"Can't tell you." She winked. Helping me get dressed and into my wheelchair, she pushed me out of my room.

"You know what it is, don't you?" I asked her.

"Yup!" She smiled at me.

"And so do I," another nurse said.

They were both so happy. I was so excited. It was so nice they were doing something for me. And my day got even better.

"What are you doing here?" I tried to get up after spotting him from down the hall, but I was too weak to stand.

"I wanted to say happy birthday! I told you I would stop by!" Chris said while fist bumping me. "What, did you think I would forget?"

"I thought you would have come earlier. I thought you weren't coming. Isn't it almost game time? Shouldn't you be there already? What time is it?" I tried to find a clock.

"Oh, that. Yeah, you're coming with me."

I looked up at him, then at Danielle. I was confused.

"But I can't; Zoe said I'm too sick to go to any games." I sulked and looked down at my feet. "And who would I sit with?"

"Well," Chris knelt down next to me. "Dr. Sheehan is a really cool doctor, and she said you are okay to go! What the doctor says goes, right?" He smiled.

"That's right, Gabe. I don't think a few hours will hurt. I'm going to go with you to make sure you are okay! It's going to be a fun night."

"Is this for real? Like, I'm not dreaming?" I hit myself in the forehead.

"Yes, Gabe, this is for real," Chris said with a little laughter in his voice.

"Oh my God, this is so exciting! I'm going to my first game! I'll get to see you play for real!" I couldn't stop saying it.

"Well, come on, I've got to get to the arena! Let's go, bud!"

Danielle pushed my wheelchair out of the hospital and hooked me up to a small IV that we could easily attach to the wheelchair.

This is going to be the best birthday I've ever had!

{33}

Christian

"We are definitely going to the arena, right?" Gabe sat anxiously in the back seat.

"Unless you want to go somewhere else?" I looked back at him through the rearview mirror.

"Nope. I'm good."

"I figured." Laughing, I made the turn to the arena.

"Wow! Look at all of the people walking in!" His eyes were wide with curiosity and excitement. He didn't even know half of what his day was going to entail.

I reached underneath my jacket, and my fingers latched onto the chain I opened earlier. If only James was here to witness all of this. I know he would have taken just as much of a liking to Gabe as I have. Being able to give Gabe a night like tonight very much resembled something that James would have done for me.

When we got out of the car, Danielle and I put Gabe in the wheelchair and made sure he was comfortable. We parked in the back so we could enter by the locker rooms. This way we wouldn't risk anyone who may know Zoe seeing Gabe, or worse, seeing Zoe before it was the right time.

"So where are our seats? Does Zoe know I'm here?"

"No, she doesn't. This is a surprise for her too. But your seats, well, you have the best seat in the house." I winked.

"Where's that?" Gabe's eyes lit up with pure joy.

"You'll see. First we have to make a pit stop to the locker room."

"The locker room? We are going to *the locker room?*" Gabe yelled and almost jumped out of his wheelchair. His reaction was priceless. Emotions ran through me like a wildfire. I looked at Gabe and realized I cared more about him than I did my own self. He was family to me now.

"Oh my God. I'm going in the locker room. Will the whole team be in there?" I nodded. "Oh my God. I'm going in the locker room." Gabe whispered to himself over and over again. Danielle and I looked at each other, and the two of us could hardly contain our laughter.

"Are you ready?" I looked down at Gabe. He looked a little nervous as we got closer.

"Yes! But wait, sorry, Danielle. I don't think you can come in. Boys only."

"Yes, I'll wait right out here!" Danielle chuckled.

"Hey, before we go in there, I want to give you something." I choked up a bit.

"What's that?"

I reached around the back of my neck, and my trembling thumbs tried to unhook the clasp to my chain.

"Here, why don't I help you?" Danielle took notice to the emotions that were becoming hard to control. Placing it in my hand, I bent down next to Gabe.

"This…this I just got as a gift, and now I want to give it to you." I stared down at the palm of my hand.

"But if it was given to you, why are you giving it to me?" he questioned.

"It is very special to me, and I want you to take good care of it."

I looked at Gabe and smiled.

"This was given to me by my brother, and now it's yours."

"Your brother? You have a brother?"

"I did. You know how you told me your Daddy is in heaven?" Gabe nodded. "Well, my brother is there with him. I know he would want you to have it."

"Are you sure?"

I nodded.

"Wow."

We remained silent for a few moments while Gabe examined the chain. Danielle turned away and wiped her eyes.

"Can you put it on me?"

"I would love to." I stood up and wrapped it around his neck. "What do you say? Time to go meet all the guys?" I tried to change the momentum.

"Yes! I'm ready!"

I opened the door, and all of the guys stood there and giving Gabe a welcome he will never forget. One of my teammates was holding a balloon, and Matt was holding a jersey we had designed just for him to wear. After explaining to Matt what was going on, we were able to put our differences behind us.

"We've been waiting all day for you!" Matt yelled.

"This is awesome!" Gabe said while looking up at me. My heart was beating out of my chest. I couldn't hold back the tears any longer. But my nerves for seeing how Zoe would react disappeared. This is going to be perfect. There's no way something could go wrong now.

"So we have something for you. We had this made especially for you to wear tonight." Matt turned the jersey around, and it had Gabe's name on the back. "How would you like to be a part of the team today?"

"Are you serious? Is he serious?" Gabe looked back up at me. "Are you serious?" he repeated quietly.

"So serious!" I put my hand on his shoulder.

"Give me that jersey!" The guys laughed and all smiled.

"So where is my new player?" Coach Higgins walked into the locker room.

"Are you ready to be a Saint for the day?" He shook Gabe's hand.

"Yes! Thank you!" He toned his excitement down a notch, maybe out of nervousness from being in the presence of the coach. He could be a little intimidating.

"No need to thank me. We are so glad to have you here with us today. And happy birthday! How old are you now?"

"I'm nine! Next year I'll be in the double digits!"

"Happy birthday!" One of my teammates walked over and gave Gabe a high five.

"Thank you!" His smile got wider.

"Hey, kiddo. So glad to have you with us today! Happy birthday!" Another teammate gave him a fist bump.

One by one they each made their way over to individually speak with him. Watching Gabe in this moment was like watching his sickness slip out from underneath his skin and float up into the sky. The inner demon that was slowly killing him seemed to completely disappear. He was full of life for the first time since I met him.

{34}

Gabe

My wheelchair was parked in the corner of the locker room. I watched as the guys put their good sneakers on and got ready for the game. Some, after talking to me, put headphones in. There was so much green and gold in here. It was even better than I imagined it would look.

I went to scratch my neck, and my finger touched the new necklace Chris gave me. It was so nice. He was sitting next to me on the floor stretching. I looked down at him and thought about how sad it must make him that his brother is in heaven like my dad.

"Taking it all in?" he asked.

"Can I ask you a question?"

"Ask away!" He reached his hand down to his toes.

"Do you think your brother knows my dad?"

He just stared at me when I asked.

"You know, since they're both in heaven?"

"I bet they do."

"Was your brother as cool as you? Because if I go to heaven, Zoe said I'll get to meet my dad, so maybe I'll get to meet your brother too." Knowing that all of these people were in heaven made me feel better. I was scared I would be alone but now I know I won't be.

"What are you talking about? Christian is far from being cool." His teammate Matt sat down next to me, laughing.

When I woke up this morning I didn't think my day would be like this. I didn't think I would be spending my birthday with my favorite team. This birthday is awesome!

"Thank you for the best birthday present ever!" I thanked Chris.

"It was my idea." Matt said, and Chris hit him. "No, it was his idea. He's really nice, isn't he?"

"He's my best friend," I agreed with Matt, and for some reason he looked like he was going to cry.

"When am I going to see Zoe? I can't wait to show her my jersey!" I asked.

"She's meeting us down here in just a few minutes! Do you think she'll be excited?"

"Oh, yes! She'll probably be so excited to see me!"

"I hope she won't be mad." Christian said.

"Tell her to suck it up if she is."

A few minutes later after listening to Coach Higgins talk to the team, we were headed out of the locker room. Chris was pushing me behind everybody. It was almost game time.

"Okay, so are you okay? You're going to be going out on the court with all of us," he asked me.

"I'm okay. I won't be nervous," I lied. I wasn't a little kid anymore. I could handle it.

We entered into the hallway behind the arena, and that's when I spotted Zoe.

I looked up at Chris as soon as we saw her because he stopped walking. He looked so nervous, but he smiled so big. You could tell that he liked her a lot by the way he looked at her. I think he may even love her.

"Zoe!" I shouted and waved to her anxiously.

This is the best day ever! I didn't want the night to end.

{35}

Zoe

I looked at my phone. It was almost game time. So far I've answered the phone once. Wrong number. Of course. I couldn't be any more bored. By now all of my nail polish was chipped off into a small pile on the desk in front of me. I had my grocery list and my to-do list for school written out, and I read through today's paper.

I don't even know why it's necessary that I am up here. Who is going to call during the game? Why wouldn't they just go to the customer service booth or call the box office? What was the point of me being here?

My cell phone rang.

"Ugh, it's so boring up here. Please tell me you're coming up here!"

"No, but we need you down here by the locker room, like, ASAP." Emily said frantically.

"I don't think I can leave." I was confused.

"Yes, you can. I was given specific orders to tell you."

"Oh, that's weird. What do you need me for?"

"I'm not exactly sure, but I'm headed there now. She said that gray door by the bathroom in the office leads to a hallway that will bring you down here. It's a quicker way, so just go down those stairs, I guess."

"Okay, I'll hang up and be right down."

"Okay, hurry!"

By the locker room. Does this mean I'll see Christian?

My hands were trembling, and my entire original plan of what I wanted to say to him went flying out the window. I wouldn't be able to talk to him now anyway. But even if I was, even if for some odd chance I would be able to, I would probably be too nervous. I should have written it all down to give to him instead.

Rushing through the office, I found the gray door she was talking about. It really was a much quicker way. I wonder why I've never noticed this before. I was going down the stairs so fast I almost slipped and fell. It sounded urgent, and I didn't want to make my boss mad. Turning around the corner toward the locker room, I stood still. I couldn't breathe. It felt like my chest was going to explode. I closed my eyes.

My feet were stuck to the ground beneath me. I was frozen. Re-opening my eyes slowly, I confirmed that I was indeed really seeing this. It wasn't just a hallucination from being dehydrated. I wasn't going crazy.

"What are you doing here?" I yelled to Gabe, and I walked, well, ran toward him and Christian.

In that moment I forgot Christian was standing there with Gabe. The look on Gabe's face said it all. I have never seen him this way before. Happiness was drawn all over his face.

I got anxious, and it hit me. *What is going on?* I thought.

"I'm a Saint for the day! How awesome is this? Best birthday ever!" Gabe exclaimed loudly.

I knelt down next to him and gave him a kiss on the forehead.

"I love you, buddy." I was teary eyed. I know how I'm feeling right now, so I can't even begin to imagine how he is feeling, but I have a pretty good guess.

"Look at this!" Gabe held up a chain that laid on his chest. "He gave this to me too. His brother gave this to him. His brother is in heaven with Daddy."

I stood up and made eye contact with Christian for the first time in weeks.

"What is all of this? Is this what you couldn't tell me?" I whispered.

"Sort of, yeah. We aren't finished yet." Christian smirked and looked over at Danielle.

"You knew about this too?"

"Yes, I did. The entire staff did, actually!" she smiled.

"It's good to see you," I said to Christian.

"You too, but we can talk later. Gabe, are you ready?"

"Ready for..." He looked up at Christian with a huge grin.

"For the game! Let's go!" Christian pushed Gabe toward the tunnel to get onto the court. The team was jumping up and down to their entrance music that was playing.

"Zoe, follow us." He looked back at me. I stood there in shock, still trying to process what was going on. I couldn't even get a word in before the team ran out, and before I knew it, we were on the edge of the court.

The arena was packed. I don't think there was an empty seat, and we haven't had a sell-out game all season. Before I was finished looking around at my surroundings, the lights went out.

"Okay, so they're going to call me out there, and then you'll know what to do." He whispered in my ear.

Christian proceeded to go out to the center of the court where he met his parents for Senior Recognition Day. Coach Higgins recognized him along with the Director of Athletics for all of the success he has brought to the Saints during his career on the team. The announcer handed him a microphone and everyone but Christian walked off of the court.

Is this all a dream? I couldn't figure out how this all happened right under my nose.

"Thank you, Siena fans, for all of the support these last four years. It's been an amazing ride, and I couldn't do it without all of you. As much as I appreciate everyone coming here for senior night, tonight is not my night. We're all here tonight for a special friend of mine."

Christian looked over at us. Even though he was far away, I could see how much he cared for Gabe. The love radiated off of him and was visible in his voice.

"My buddy Gabe is here, and today is his birthday. At just nine years old, he's been suffering from an aggressive form of leukemia for a few years now. So today, we are all here to give him the biggest birthday party he's ever had. I want to thank everyone who helped plan this or came out to celebrate with us! Up until right now, he and his sister—my girlfriend,"

Girlfriend. He said girlfriend. I can't even breathe right now. Staring over at Christian, the only thoughts going through my mind right now is how could I have gotten this lucky to have him in my life...*how were Gabe and I so lucky?*

"They had no idea about any of this. So today, Gabe is not only getting the biggest surprise party of his life, but he's going to be a Saint for the day. So come on, everyone! Let's all cheer him on! Everyone, welcome Gabe Gingras!"

The crowd went insane. Everything remained dark, and a spotlight was the only form of light. Soon the quiet arena filled with a booming applause and cheers. Lacey walked over to center court, and Christian handed her the microphone.

"Hi, everyone! If anyone doesn't know me, my name is Lacey, and I'm the cheer captain for the Saints. When Chris came to me with this idea and asked to get me on board to present it to Athletics, I couldn't refuse. I met a lot of you at the doors today, and I want to thank each and every one of you for your support. In conjunction to this being his party, we also decided to help his family. As most of you know, medical treatments can be very costly. Everything we've raised will go directly toward Gabe's medical care.

We don't have an exact total yet, but we are estimating that from tonight and in the weeks prior we've raised a total of over $100,000!"

"Did she just say..." I almost lost my balance. Danielle grabbed my hand and gripped it tighter.

"Yes, I think she did," Danielle replied.

"Holy shit." I gasped. My heart was racing.

Lacey continued.

"If you gave a donation before the event or at the door, you were given a glow stick. If you have one, it's now time to break it. Can we turn the spotlight off, please? Let's light up Gabe's world."

All at once, green and yellow lights lit up until it appeared to be that the entire arena was lit. Tears were streaming down my cheeks. Danielle handed me a tissue out of her purse. Spinning around to take this all in, I watched the continuous lights appear. This is unreal.

I bent down next to Gabe and noticed that he was now crying.

"Are you okay, buddy?"

"This is all for me? Everyone here did this for me? All for me?"

"Yes, buddy, it is." I held his hand and watched him look around at the lit up arena. To see how much support we had in the Siena community was unimaginable, especially since they don't even know us. Then I thought, *how did I not hear about any of this?*

"Zoe. This is the best day of my life." Gabe's words nearly broke my heart.

I looked up on the court where Christian was motioning for me to bring Gabe out. The team lined up on either side, making a tunnel for him to go through, and I watched him signal to the desk.

"And now, ladies and gentlemen, the moment we have all been waiting for. Let me introduce to you the newest Siena Saint, number 3, Gabe Gingras!"

The crowd went wild. The lights spiraled around the arena and all of the glow sticks were dancing around in the air. I swear the arena was rocking from people's feet that were stomping the ground forcefully. Endless cheering and clapping surrounded us. The pep band played "When the Saints Go Marching In" loudly. I pushed Gabe through the tunnel, and each teammate high fived him and followed us out to center court where we met Christian.

He grabbed my hand when I approached him. I looked around as the lights came on and everyone stood up. His parents, standing at the edge of the court, waved to me and smiled. His mom was crying, and his dad held her closely. Lacey stood beside him, and I didn't know what else to do but hug her. It was evident I was wrong about her and about Christian's intentions with her.

"Thank you," I whispered to her.

We were about to head off of the court, but through the dark I could make out that a man was slowly approaching us. I thought the surprises were all over. From the looks of it, Christian did too.

The Director of Athletics met us out on the court and grabbed the microphone.

"When Christian and Lacey came to me with this idea, I wanted to be a part of it. I knew about Gabe's condition because his sister Zoe works for our department. I, however, wasn't aware of how severe it was until a few weeks ago. I'm here to present Gabe with two things. One, Gabe, it's nice to meet you."

"You too," Gabe shyly said. I don't think he knew how to react since he was so overwhelmed.

"Tonight you are a Saint for the day. But, if you accept, I want to offer you a permanent spot on the team. How would you like to be a Saint for life?"

I held Christian's hand tighter.

"I didn't know about this part," he whispered in my ear and kissed my cheek.

"I love you," I responded and looked down at Gabe. He looked like he was about to jump out of his skin. He turned to me.

"Don't get mad at me or try and stop me. Please."

"What—"

Before I could ask, Gabe rose from the wheelchair. Christian instinctively stood beside him to offer to help him up, but he didn't want it. He pushed his hand out of the way and stood up with both feet on the ground. He shook the Director's hand.

"Where do I sign the contract?" He said right into the microphone.

The crowd laughed and all applauded as he handed Gabe a certificate, which stated that he was a Saint for life.

"Second, Zoe, our department did a little fundraising on our own, and we want to thank our major sponsors for coming together to support this cause. We are going to be able to match what they've raised."

Oh my God. For the last ten minutes, all I wanted to do was pinch myself. I thought if I did I would wake up, find that this was all a dream. This was too good to be true. This couldn't be real. But it was. I don't know how it happened, and I never expected that the community, my friends, and the school would put time and effort in to help save my little brothers life.

Right then, God answered so many of my prayers. I'd never felt more loved. I had all I could ever need. With all this money, Gabe was going to be able to get his full treatment and anything else necessary to help him recover. Gabe would have a much greater chance of surviving this. He could beat his battle.

The game was about to start, and we had to exit the court. Christian showed us to our seats that were right behind the team bench. I turned to Christian.

"Now it's your night. Kick ass."

He smiled at me, pulled me in tight, and gave me a quick kiss. In those three seconds, I knew that I wanted to be with him for the rest of my life.

{36}

Christian

"Son, I am so very proud of you. You have grown up into such an amazing man, and to see what you did tonight—"

My dad choked up on his words. I have never seen him like this before. The only time I've seen him cry was at James' funeral.

I walked my parents out to their car as they were leaving the hospital to head to the hotel. After meeting Zoe and Gabe, they decided they were going to stick around for a few days and booked a hotel room.

My mom grabbed me and hugged me tight. "Your brother would have been so proud. You are such a caring person, and you just helped to save a child's life."

"I'm hoping I will actually be able to save his life."

"What do you mean?" My dad asked.

"They think I might be a match for bone marrow. I've been undergoing tests for weeks now to see if I would be a good donor."

My parents stared at me.

"Zoe doesn't know. I didn't want to say anything until I know for sure. I don't want to get her hopes up."

My mom latched onto my dad's hand. It was evident that tonight was an emotional rollercoaster for them as well.

"I really like her. Zoe, I mean. She is so strong for what she has gone through, and she's so in love with you. She looks at you like the way I looked at your father."

The tears were streaming down my mom's face. I couldn't keep myself composed either.

"I love her. So much. So, so much, Mom. I don't want to see her go through any more pain. I don't want her to lose Gabe."

"I know, honey. I know."

"You're doing amazing things for them. You're doing the right thing," My dad whispered in agreement.

"We're going to stick around for a while. I want to help too." My mom wiped her eyes with her sleeve.

"Oh, you don't have to do that."

"But we want to—or at least I will, for as long as you or Zoe need. Even if it's just to cook a dinner once in a while or keep her company."

"You just want to get to know Zoe, don't you?" I threw in some humor to lighten the mood.

"Well of course! But you know what I mean."

"I do. Thank you, Mom. I'm sure she is going to appreciate it." I leaned in to give her a hug goodbye.

Waving goodbye to my parents as they drove off into the darkness, I walked back into the hospital to get Zoe.

"Almost ready to go?" I popped into Gabe's room.

"Yeah. Gabe, you have had quite the day today! You need to get some rest now. Christian is going to take me home, but—"

"I'm going to stay here with you tonight, so I'll be back!"

"Best birthday ever," Gabe shouted again with excitement.

"We know." Zoe and I both laughed. He'd been repeating that statement all day. She gave him a kiss on the forehead, and we headed toward the exit. Her hand in mine, life couldn't get much better than this.

"I really missed you," she said.

I quickly turned my head to get a glimpse of the happiness that I could hear in her voice.

"I missed that smile."

"So Lacey really helped? That was why you were meeting with her? I'm sorry I jumped to conclusions. I just never thought—"

"I know. I'm sorry I lied. I just didn't know what to tell you if I told you I was meeting her in the first place. I wanted to keep this night a surprise. So that's why I didn't tell you."

"I understand now. Really. I just wish we could make up for the lost time."

"I'm not going anywhere," I reassured her.

Pulling into her driveway, I put the car in park. Silence filled the air. I came clean about lying to her, but not entirely.

"You sure you don't want to come in?" she asked.

"It's tempting, but I'm sure. I want to get back to the hospital and catch Gabe before he falls asleep. He's definitely had a long day."

"You are my hero. You know that?" Zoe smiled. She was so beautiful when she smiled. I placed my hand on her cheek.

Definitely don't tell her tonight. I thought to myself.

"You are beautiful. You know that?" I couldn't stop smiling either.

"I can't believe we've gone this long without talking."

"Honestly, it's probably better we didn't talk throughout all this planning. I don't know if I could have pulled it off, even though every day I didn't talk to you or see you it killed me on the inside."

"Oh I'm sure you were just fine."

"I'm never going to leave you. I made a promise to you, and I am making that to you again right now."

"I know. I'm never going to leave you either."

"I love you, Zoe Elizabeth Gingras."

"I love you, Christian Ryan Michaels." I loved the way she gazed into my eyes while those words rolled off of her tongue.

Life was perfect. A little too perfect. I felt as if things couldn't be this right in the world for long.

{37}

Gabe
One Week Later

"So where are you going?"

"Out with Emily," Zoe yelled through the closed bathroom door.

"So why are you getting yourself all pretty then?" She was taking an awfully long time in the bathroom. I think she has brought her whole drawer of make-up to my hospital room by now.

"Can't I look nice for a night?" She opened the door and popped her head out. Her hair was on top of her head in a messy bun.

"You always look nice," I wheezed. It was a little hard for me to breathe.

"You okay?" Zoe looked concerned.

"Yeah, I'm fine. Just thirsty."

"Good! I don't want to have to worry!" She shut the door again.

I stared at the closed door. I didn't want her to worry either. She always worried.

Looking over at my cup of water, it looked much farther away than it was. I tried to sit up but my back felt like it weighed a lot.

"I just can't wait for tonight. It's going to be so much fun. It's been so long since I've gone out or even had a girls' night with Emily." Her voice was loud even though the door was shut.

It made me really happy to see how happy Zoe is. She seemed really excited for tonight. I was thinking that it probably would make her sad if I told her I wasn't feeling good.

So I just won't tell her.

"Are you going to be okay here by yourself until Christian gets here? You're lucky he's coming to see you the night before the big game! Don't forget to wish him luck. I really hope they win."

I reached for my cup of water, but it wasn't easy.

"Yeah, I will be, and I won't forget. Zoe, they'll win the championship. They always do with Christian."

My hand was around the cup, but it was hard to grab it. The feeling in my hands was starting to go, and it felt as if none of the muscles in my arms were working. It was scaring me.

I stared at the door. I couldn't tell Zoe. I couldn't. She's been so happy. I couldn't ruin this night for her. I'll be fine.

God please let me be fine. I don't want Zoe to worry.

Finally wrapping my fingers around the cup, I brought it in closer to me. Tilting my head down, I moved the cup closer to my lips. The cup was shaking, and before I could get a sip, it just fell out of my hand. Water spilled all over my shirt.

I hurriedly moved my blanket up to my chin. I didn't want Zoe to see the mess I've made. She would probably wonder what was wrong.

The wet shirt made my skin cold. I buried myself as far under the blanket as I could to stay warm now too.

"What do you think?"

Zoe walked out of the bathroom.

"Wow. You look really pretty!" I tried to fight back my tears. I was scared. Something was really wrong, but I couldn't ruin her night.

"Are you sure it's okay I leave for the night?"

"Yes. I'm tired anyways. I'm just going to sleep."

"Okay. But you know I hate leaving you."

"I know. I love you, Zoe."

"Aw, Gabe, I love you too!"

She grabbed her purse, and I watched as she walked out the door.

"God, please help me. Please let me be okay," I prayed and rubbed my thumb and index finger around the necklace that Chris got me.

{38}

Zoe

I bragged to Emily about how well things were going with Christian now as we sat up at the bar. I haven't really seen much of her since the game because of all the excitement.

"So what were his parents like?"

"They are really nice! They're still here actually!"

"What, really? Why?" She was shocked.

"His mom has been so helpful! They wanted to stay around to help, I guess." I took a huge sip of my margarita.

"Yes! That's good! I've always found that meeting the parents is very nerve wracking."

"Well, it also helped I was in an entire other world when I met them, considering—"

"Yes, true! I still cannot believe how that all went down! He told me about it two days before, and I had to bite my lip every time I talked to you!"

"What! I can't believe *you* were able to keep a secret like that!" Emily couldn't ever keep a secret.

"I know! Me too! I'm proud of myself."

"Was it wrong of me to leave Gabe tonight?"

"No, don't start with that. You know he'll be fine." Emily reassured me.

"I just feel so guilty when I leave him." I sighed.

"Ladies, what can I get you?" the bartender interrupted while staring at our almost empty glasses.

"Two double shots of Fireball and two Bacardi's with pineapple."

"Woah! Look who's back in the game!" Emily laughed.

"Hey, I can drink every once in a while!"

"I know. I just haven't seen this side of you in a long time."

The bartender laid the shots down in front of us.

"To happiness!" I held up the shot glass.

"To happiness!" Emily touched hers against mine, and then we both threw it back.

"Ugh." I swallowed deeply and drank a sip of my drink. "Maybe we should have done single shots."

"I'm just so happy you are happy."

"Me too." I started to think about everything.

"I just can't get over last week. Sometimes I still cry happy tears thinking about it. How lucky am I to find a guy like him? He's so good to Gabe and me for everything that is going on in our life. Ugh, here I go."

"Oh my God, stop crying. We're out at a bar," Emily joked.

"I'm sorry! I can't help it!"

"I'm just kidding. I know. I don't know how I would have acted if I were you. It's really amazing everything that he did. Seriously though, the amount of money that has been raised too!"

"I know! Plus it just keeps coming. I went to the bank with Christian the other day, and we opened up a separate account just for donations. But Emily, now I don't have anything to worry about! I'm still so overwhelmed. It's still so hard to believe."

"The power of kindness is truly amazing."

My phone started going off, interrupting our conversation. As I answered and listened to what was being said on the other end, I don't know if I was in more shock, or if the alcohol was starting to get to me, but I had to run to the garbage to throw up.

"Emily, we need to leave. We need to leave, like, right now."

"Do you seriously have that low of a tolerance?"

"It's Gabe."

I stared at Emily with great despair, but she pushed me out the door and quickly was able to flag down a cab.

I watched the other cars drive by and the scenery of the trees through the window. I thought the day my father died would be the only day I would feel like this, but just like that, within seconds, my entire world had shut down again.

{39}

Christian

I had an entire night planned out for us. I was going to take him to the basketball court, out in back of the hospital to shoot a few baskets with his friend Johnny, and then we were going to spend the rest of the night watching some of the greatest sports movies. I had no idea that tonight was going to end up how it did.

I sat outside of the room speechless. I couldn't breathe; I couldn't think; I couldn't even bear to call Zoe myself and tell her the news.

I continued to replay what happened in my mind. I couldn't stop thinking about it. I couldn't stop wondering if there was something I could have done to prevent this from happening.

We were all set to go outside. I walked out of the room to talk to Danielle while Gabe used the bathroom. I was gone for not even five minutes, but when I came back, there he was, on the ground beside the bed.

"I need some help in here! Someone help!" I yelled out into the hallway as I bent down beside him on the ground.

"Please don't go. Hang on, buddy. Hang on. Do it for Zoe. You're strong." I bent over him. His face was pressed up against the floor, and his body was limp. The doctors, nurses, and some staff ran in and started to push me out of the way.

One of the nurses pushed me out of the room and then shut the door in my face. I paced back and forth before I was able to sit down.

Twenty minutes have gone by, and Zoe still wasn't here yet. *Where was she?* I was panicking. Sharp pains were present throughout my entire body, and I started to have an anxiety attack.

Dr. Sheehan opened the door and pulled her mask down. "Is Zoe here yet?"

"Not yet. Is he okay? What's going on?" I could barely speak.

"I think I'd better wait for Zoe."

"No, I need to know, especially if it's urgent."

"It's getting bad. I need you to get down to the lab ASAP to have your blood tested again. He needs surgery tonight. He needs a stem cell transplant too."

"What if I don't have strong enough test results?" I couldn't grasp what was going on.

"Well, he's still on the transplant list, and in that we'll continue to search. Your DNA was a match. We just need to see if you have a high enough white blood cell count, among other things, to know if it would work."

"What if my numbers are close? Can we still do it just to try?"

"I'm afraid not. If his body ever rejects the bone marrow...well, just get down there now and get tested."

I stood there and stared. What if his body rejected the bone marrow anyway?

"Go! Get moving! We need to hurry!" Dr. Sheehan pushed me down the hall. She explained the process if I were to be the perfect match. While passing Gabe's room, I took a peek inside. He was hooked up to even more machines now, and his body was close to the color of his white pillows.

"Hang in there, Gabe. I'm going to save your life," I whispered and then continued to follow the doctor down the hallway.

"God, please let me save his life," I said aloud.

{40}

Zoe

I ran into the hospital faster than I've ever run before. If I were in a race right now, I probably would have won. Getting the news that your brother collapsed will make you sober up real quick. Arriving at his room, I stopped outside the door and stared in. He wasn't awake, and the nurses were drawing more blood. I cried heavily.

"Where's Christian?" My voice screeched when I spoke to Danielle, who was standing in the corner away from the other doctors. Her hand covered her mouth and her other dabbed her now teary eyes. Since she was so personally invested in Gabe's life, the staff wouldn't allow her to work on him anymore for fear her attachment would prevent her from doing her best job.

She looked around. "I actually don't know." She gasped. "He was standing right outside, I thought."

I couldn't sit still.

"Can someone please tell me what's going on? Is Gabe going to be okay? Please tell me!"

Just then, I spotted Dr. Sheehan coming around the corner, and then I heard my name being called from the other direction. It was Christian's mom. I looked at her and then ran toward Dr. Sheehan.

"How is he? What's going on? Don't leave anything out."

"To get right to the point, he needs a bone marrow transplant immediately. We think we have a match. We are just doing further testing to be sure."

I broke down. "How am I not a match? I'm his family. It doesn't make any sense. Test me again!"

"Zoe, that unfortunately can happen. This happens all the time. Family members aren't always a match." Dr. Sheehan put her hand on my shoulder. "We are going to do everything we can."

"Where the hell is my mom? Where in this world is she? Why isn't she here saving her own son's life?" I wiped the hateful tears from my eyes. Emily stood on one side of me and Christian's mom to the other side. They both looked very distraught.

"Let me know as soon as you hear anything, please. He's the only family I have left." I tried to calm myself down.

"I will."

I turned around, and Christian's mom embraced me, and I wept in her arms.

"Where's Christian?"

"Wait, you didn't see him? He's the one who called me to tell me."

"No, I got here and he wasn't in the room. No one seems to know where he is." I grabbed a tissue from the table next to us and blew my nose.

"He found him. I can't imagine it was easy for him. He'll show up soon. The night we found out about James, he disappeared for a while. It's how he deals with things like this. Here, come with me." She grabbed my hand and walked me down the hallway.

We entered into the chapel where we sat in an all too familiar pew.

"This is where I sat when my dad was dying. I prayed and prayed and prayed, but he didn't make it." I sighed.

I couldn't stop crying even if I tried. I haven't even told Christian the details from when my father died, but somehow I was finding it easy to trust his mother.

"I find comfort in God's presence. But Zoe, Gabe will survive this. They'll find a match real soon. I know they will. Can I show you something?"

"Yeah, sure." I wiped my eyes with my sleeve and grabbed another tissue. I was getting very congested from all of the crying.

His mom opened her purse and pulled something out. It looked like it was a picture, but she stared at the back of it for quite some time before turning it over.

"I carry this with me everywhere I go. It's a picture of the boys. It was taken the day before we lost James. We took it on the quad when James moved in. Did my boy ever tell you the full story of what happened?"

"No, he didn't. We haven't really talked about the details of my father's death much or his brother's, just that they're no longer with us."

"We had just left him at school. We didn't leave the area, but we had just said goodbye. A few of his roommates went out drinking that night and asked for him to pick them up. Since he always wanted to be a good friend and put others first, he didn't refuse. He was headed to pick them up when he saw a car on the side of the road with its lights flashing. Luckily, he brought a friend he had just met with him who could tell me exactly what happened that night. He went to the car to see if the people needed any help. The man in the driver's seat appeared to have had a heart attack."

The story sounded all too familiar to me. *It couldn't be.*

"They didn't know how long he was sitting there before they found him. James went to go run back to the car to grab his phone to call 911, and as he was running toward the car," she paused, "a drunk driver came around the corner."

She flipped the picture around and I stared at the picture before me. I looked at the two boys, one of whom had a face I have never been able to forget. I replayed what she was saying over and over in my head. I replayed everything that has happened between Christian and me. I replayed the night my father died over and over.

I looked over to the pew I sat in that very night. I closed my eyes and the memories came flashing back to me. I remembered the way he held my hand when I started to cry, how there was a sense of calmness in his voice, and how even through a dark time, he somehow managed to make me smile.

That little boy who consoled me as my father was dying in the hospital, the boy who remained anonymous to me—it was Christian. Which meant the young man who tried to save my father's life, who gave me those few last few minutes with my father, was James.

I looked up at the cross on the altar and then did what I only knew to do in that moment—pray.

{41}

Christian

I waited in suspense for the results while sitting outside of the exam room. My mind was running endlessly. I knew I should be back by Gabe with Zoe, but I didn't want her to know what I was doing in case I wasn't going to be a match good enough. Hopefully my mom was there by now to help out if she needed anything.

"Chris?"

"Yeah." I lifted my head up, and Dr. Sheehan was standing over me. "Did you get the results?"

"If we do this, you are going to have to rest for two days, which means you won't be able to play in the game."

"No, I'm going to do this. It's just a game."

"Are you sure? Do you want to call your coach? It's a pretty big game. Isn't it the championship game?"

"Yeah, I'll handle it. Does that mean I'm a match?"

"Yes. You are a match and everything looks like it would be perfect. I can't even believe it. I don't know how, but you are." Dr. Sheehan was muttering. I don't think she was handling this very well either.

I stood up. "Great, let's go then. Let's save his life."

"Alright then. Tracy, take Mr. Michaels and get him prepped. Tell my staff to meet me in OR 2 for a bone marrow transplant." She spoke over to the nurse behind the desk handing her paperwork to fill out.

I took a deep breath. On the walk with the nurse, I picked up my phone and called my coach.

"It's Michaels. I can't play in the game. Put Smith in instead. He deserves playing time. I'm about to save Gabe's life. I'll be watching. Win it for Gabe."

I left the message on his voicemail.

This was going to work. This had to work. Gabe needed to survive this. He needed to beat this. After everything, he had to. He just had to. I walked into the exam room, where Tracy handed me a hospital gown and started to do a write up.

"Put this on, and I'll be right back so we can get started shortly." She spoke as she shut the door behind her.

The events of tonight reminded me of the picture I saw on Zoe's nightstand. I recognized that little girl in the picture from the chapel that very night. I didn't even know how to bring it up to Zoe since I found it.

It blows my mind that neither of us had figured it out before. Did Zoe have any suspicions about it? Did she know, and was she also afraid to bring it up? It was honestly hard for me to comprehend.

I'm not sure what I believe right now, if this was all just a coincidence or if God placed us in each other's lives for a reason. Was I always meant to save Gabe? If James hadn't saved her father's life, would I have even met her? If James didn't die that night, would I have even gone to Siena? Since James saved her dad's life, why wouldn't I be able to save Gabe's?

I sat here trembling. The many thoughts that flooded my mind brought me to tears. I wanted to tell Zoe about this so bad. I wanted to be with her right now more than anything. Holding her close and rubbing her back, telling her that everything would be okay.

Right now she needed me more than ever, and she probably thinks I abandoned her during an incredibly difficult time. But right at this moment, I was in the same position as my brother was several years ago. I had a chance to save Gabe's life and to save this family.

{42}

Zoe

Some days I think are the worst days of my life. I've had several of those in my lifetime. But right now? Right now tops how I've felt in all of those moments. This has been the most difficult time of my entire life. I constantly worried if Gabe was going to survive this. Was this going to work? The only thing keeping my mind off of Gabe was my recent discovery.

Walking back from the chapel, Emily ran up to me.

"Where have you been? Dr. Sheehan was just looking for you."

"Is everything okay?" She scared me.

"I don't know! She said she would check to see if you were back in a minute." Emily was panicked.

I paced back and forth. Did she have good news? Was it more bad news? I'm not sure I could take any more bad news.

Looking up from my feet, I noticed that Dr. Sheehan was walking straight toward me, and Mrs. Michaels grabbed my hand.

"How is he? Is he okay?"

"There's been no change in his condition. I'm sorry."

"That's it?" I was confused.

"No, I have good news." Dr. Sheehan pulled down her mask and Emily came closer.

"We have a match. We're pulling Gabe in for surgery now."

"Oh my God." I cried hysterically in Mrs. Michaels' arms, who had also begun crying. Emily stood behind me and rubbed my arm.

"Are you sure this is going to work?"

"I promise you that we're going to do everything we can."

Before she walked away, I could have sworn I saw a tear fall from her eyes. Knowing Dr. Sheehan cared about Gabe as an individual, as more than just her patient, helped me trust her.

"I'll go call Janice for you to let her know." Emily took her phone out of her pocket and walked a few feet away.

"Thank you."

I sat down to catch my breath, to let this all settle in.

Where was Christian? I was restless, waiting for him. I needed him right here with me. But there was no sign of him anywhere. He couldn't have left. Where could he be?

The effects of the alcohol were wearing off, and my anxiety was at its highest. I needed Gabe to fight. I needed him to fight harder than he ever has before. It killed me that I couldn't do anything for him. In times like these, I needed my parents.

I gently leaned my head on Christian's mom's shoulder and held Emily's hand as she sat down. I was so grateful for them during times like these.

*

A light tapping on my shoulder awoke me from a deep sleep. When Gabe returned from surgery a few hours later, I was glued to his bedside. I must have fallen asleep with my head on his bed.

"Is everything okay?" I was startled.

I looked up, and it was Danielle.

"Zoe, come with me," she whispered.

"Wait, what? I can't leave Gabe. He's not awake yet."

"He'll be out for a little while longer. Don't worry. Everything's fine, but come with me," she insisted and walked me down the hallway to the other room. I was still half asleep and my eyes were heavy from all of the crying.

"The donor wants to talk to you."

My eyes lit up. "Wait, the donor is here, in this hospital? I just thought that they got it from some other hospital."

"Yes, he's here. Go ahead, right in there." She pointed into a room.

I walked in and then walked around the corner. I don't know how I didn't know before, but when I saw who was sitting in the bed, I cried again.

"Oh my God!" I ran up to Christian and gave him a kiss.

"Hi, beautiful," he said with groggy eyes.

"You were a match! I can't believe it. Oh my God. I can't. Wait, what? How did this happen?"

"I just hope this works."

"It will. I will never be able to repay you for this."

"You don't have to."

"Yes, I do."

The tears continued to flow down my cheeks. I didn't think I could cry anymore, but apparently I still had some tears left.

"I've been undergoing tests for weeks. Surprise." He let out a small smile.

"Is there anything else you're hiding from me?" I laughed.

"Well, there is one thing. When I was at your house a few weeks ago I saw this picture of you from when you were younger—"

I interrupted him.

"I was just sitting in the chapel with your mom. She showed me a picture of your brother and told me about the day he passed away. Then I realized."

"How didn't we know before?" His eyes locked on mine.

"It's unbelievable."

181

We sat there in silence for what seemed like a while, taking it all in. I laid by his side and he wrapped his arm tightly around my body. For a while, I forgot about all of the problems that have occurred over the last twenty-four hours.

"Can you do me a favor?"

"Yeah, what do you need?" I responded kindly.

"Can you stand over by the window for a moment and close your eyes?"

"What? Why?"

"Just do what I say, okay?" He demanded.

"What drugs do they have you on?" I laughed but obeyed his orders.

"I can't believe you are missing what could be the biggest game of your career for this."

"This was more important." I heard some movement and wanted to look. I was desired to know what he was up to.

"Okay, you can turn around now."

I spun around and wasn't expecting him to be right behind me down on his knee.

"Eight years ago, when all hope was lost in the world, when I sat in God's presence and prayed for a miracle, I prayed for happiness and for a sign that everything would be okay. Then that's when I saw you.

It may have taken us eight years to find each other again, but I believe we are right where we are supposed to be. God places people in our lives for a reason. Every moment I am with you, you make me the happiest man on earth.

I love you with all of my heart. You and Gabe are my whole life now. I can't picture another day without either of you in it. I want us to be a family. So…"

He opened his fist and held up a beautiful ring. Before he could even ask, I already knew what my answer would be.

"Will you marry me?" He asked and the room looked like it was spinning. I slowly walked backward until the back of my knees hit the chair behind me.

"I love you Zoe, I know this seems quick but when you know, you just know." He placed his hands on my knees.

"When you know what?" I said through my tears.

"When you know that you've met your soul mate."

"I love you. I love you so much." I wiped the tears away from under my eyes.

"So is that a yes?"

"My answer is yes but, only if Gabe says yes."

"I don't think he will have a problem with being my best man." Christian said as he laughed and rose up off of his knees so his face was parallel with mine.

"Me either." He kissed me softly and for the first time, I felt complete.

Epilogue
Gabe
Seven Years Later

Grabbing my permit, I raced down the stairs and through the door, almost forgetting to shut it. Janice was waiting outside in her car. She drove here the minute Chris called us. Now that we lived in a different neighborhood, she couldn't just walk over anymore.

"I'll drive! I'll drive!" I shouted to her, motioning for her to let me in the driver's seat. I got my permit only a few months back. Chris taught me how to drive, and Zoe promised that once I got my license they would get me a car. That is if I get a job. She's been driving me nuts to get one.

"No, sir. Not with me, you're not!" She gripped her hands against the steering wheel.

"Oh, come on! Chris says I'm a good driver!"

"We have to get there now! I am not letting you drive. Maybe on the way back."

I got in the passenger side of her car, and she backed out of the driveway so fast she almost hit our mailbox.

"Where were they when Chris called?"

"They just got to the hospital. He said they were taken immediately, and they didn't have to wait. I guess they were picking up flowers so we could bring them to the cemetery later."

"Oh, that's right, it's the third. Oh wow, I can't believe it's been fifteen years already. Oh my God, and today of all days!"

"I know! It's freaky right? How far away from the hospital are we?"

"Only a few more minutes. Did Chris seem nervous?"

"He definitely seemed scared, but heck, I would be too. I hope Zoe is okay!"

"She will be," Janice reassured me.

Arriving at the hospital, we raced through the doors and to the wing where Christian said they would be. I looked around at my surroundings. Even though it wasn't the same wing, I was no stranger to this hospital. It's been about five years since I've had to come back here, and it's all because of Chris. He saved my life.

When the doctors sat down with the three of us and told us I was cancer free, it was the beginning of an entire new life for us. We take a vacation every year around that date to celebrate my good health. Zoe and Christian finally got married two years ago. They were too busy starting their careers to ever plan the wedding she's always dreamed of. She wanted to wait until she finished med school. She's a doctor now, and she is going to specialize in pediatrics because of everything that happened with me. Christian started up his own non-profit that raises money for the families of sick children if they can't afford the treatments. It's pretty awesome. I help him out sometimes at the fundraisers and tell my story.

"There he is!" I shouted when I spotted Chris walking down the hallway.

"Oh, Chris! How is she?" Janice said greeting him with a hug.

"Follow me. I'll bring you to her, and you can see for yourself."

I was nervous. I don't know why. Maybe it's because I've never seen Zoe in a hospital bed before. Usually it was me and she was the one sitting at my bedside.

Walking into the room, Chris moved the curtain, revealing the bed Zoe was laying in. She was grinning from ear to ear looking down at her arms.

"This little one didn't waste any time at all making an appearance in the world," Chris said as he approached Zoe's bedside and then reached his arms out.

"It's a boy! Do you want to meet your new nephew?" Zoe asked me.

Janice walked over to Zoe and gave her a kiss on the forehead. I can't believe my sister is now a mother to her own child. She's going to make an amazing mother to her new son, just like she was for me when I was growing up. Chris approached me, and I let him place the baby in my arms.

"Hi there. I'm your Uncle Gabe. What's his name?" I turned to Chris, but I could hardly take my eyes off of my nephew. He opened his eyes and looked right up at me before letting out a big yawn.

I waited for them to announce his name. Zoe and Chris turned to each other and then back to me and Janice, who was now by my side admiring the new addition to the family.

"Well, we couldn't think of a more fitting name for this precious angel. Say hi to AJ." Chris smiled.

"Anderson James." Zoe reached for Chris's hand and he leaned down to kiss her.

"Hi, AJ. Happy birthday." I smiled.

35455319R00112

Made in the USA
San Bernardino, CA
24 June 2016